IMMEDIATE SEARCH

Book 3 of The Great Devastation Trilogy

Novels by Dana Pride

- » *Immediate Search*
- » *Hope Continually*
- » *The Hidden City*
- » *So How is THAT a Bully?*
- » *After the Great Devastation*
- » *The Red Cloak*
- » *Nightmares of Murder*
- » *No One Like You*
- » *Existing*
- » *All These Things*
- » *Kissing a Dead Man*

Non-fiction books by Dana Pride

- » *How to Get Fat Without Even Trying*
- » *What Really Happened in Mexico*
- » *We Choose our Memories: Sayings of the Young Folks*
- » *We Choose our Memories: Sayings of the Old Folks*

IMMEDIATE SEARCH

Book 3 of The Great Devastation Trilogy

BY
DANA PRIDE

Everlasting Publishing
Yakima, Washington
USA

Immediate Search

Book 3 of The Great Devastation Trilogy

by
Dana Pride

ISBN: 0-9852739-9-2

ISBN-13: 978-0-9852739-9-6

First Edition
Everlasting Publishing
P.O. Box 1061
Yakima, WA 98907

A good story needs a great ending:
Book 3 of
The Great Devastation Trilogy

For my family:

My husband, Dad, Mom, Dale, Nathan, Jahla, Akiia, Dawn, Valesia, Virgil, Willie, Delano, our 33 grandchildren and our 10 great-grandchildren.

Thank you for your encouragement all along the way.

Dana

IMMEDIATE SEARCH

After nearly nine years of living apart from her family in the utilitarian society known as the Complex, Layla found her father halfway across the world. Together they embarked on a journey that led them to her uncle. Then Layla received an encrypted message from her friend, Kenrick; a message of hope and encouragement, to initiate a search that could not wait another day.

CHAPTER 1

"I found your mother," was all that the encrypted message said.

My heart began to pound frantically. She must be still alive, somewhere, or Kenrick would not have gone to all the trouble to search for me and contact me clear on the other side of the world, cloaking his message under so many layers of code. I had to find out where she was!

I looked at my dad. I needed to get him alone so I could tell him the translation of the message. He seemed to read something on my face, but before I could say or do anything, Dawson interrupted.

"So, is this a message for you, too?" he asked sarcastically.

"Why don't you tell us all about it over dinner?" Uncle Pierce asked, gently nudging me. "Come on, let's go."

"I need to send another message," I said, reluctant to leave at this moment.

"You can send all the messages you want to send, after we eat something," Uncle Pierce said patronizingly. "I'm sure you all must be hungry."

I could tell by the look on the faces of my friends that they were probably nearly starving, although I was so excited that my stomach was one big knot. I was almost overwhelmed at the prospect of seeing my mother again.

"Daddy, can I talk to you alone for a minute?" I asked, pleading with my eyes.

"We can all talk just as much as you like when we go down to the Apple Tree Room," Uncle Pierce said, herding the group in the direction of the door. He began to lead the way.

"What is it, Layla?" my dad asked, concern filling his face.

I held back as the group moved forward, my dad staying right beside me. I stretched up to whisper in his ear.

"My friend found Mom," I said quickly. The rest of the group was not paying attention to us, as they were focusing in their upcoming meal.

"What?" my dad asked loudly, stopping in his tracks. His face was filled with a new hope, the same hope I could feel.

Uncle Pierce stopped at the door and looked back at us. I flashed him a smile, not ready to let him in on the secret just yet. He put up his hand to activate the panel that opened the door, and we followed him down the hallway, my dad and I walking a short distance behind the others.

"The message was from my friend, Kenrick, and it said, 'I found your mother.' That was it," I whispered to my dad, as the others were discussing what might be on the menu.

"What did he mean by that?" my dad asked.

"If Kenrick said that he found her, he found her! He knows where she is," I said, eager to return to the computer and send him another message.

"Let's have a nice dinner, and we can think about what to do while we eat," my dad suggested.

"I already know what to do!" I insisted.

"Things always are more clear on a full stomach," my dad said, reminding me of something my mom used to say.

He was right. At this moment, I was so tense, I was about to burst. What was I going to say to Kenrick, anyway? I needed more information in order for us to make a plan. And as I took a deep breath, my stomach growled loudly, reminding me that I was really hungry.

We quickly arrived at the Apple Tree Room, a brightly-lit, beautifully decorated eatery. The walls were made of apple trees – not real trees, but three-dimensional looking trees surrounded us. Even as we came through the door and I looked back in that direction, we seemed to have come under the branch of a tree, into an opening in the middle of an apple tree orchard. The lighting made me feel like we had stepped outside, into a patio surrounded by apple trees, in the middle of the afternoon. The apples on the trees looked real and ripe. Some were red, some were golden, and others were a mixture between red and yellow.

"They look real, don't they?" Uncle Pierce asked, observing me as I stared at the apples on the trees. "Actually, they are. You can pick one, right off the tree." He reached over to demonstrate, plucking a nice, full, red apple right off one of the fake trees.

"How you do that?" Nadir asked, staring at the apple in Uncle Pierce's hand. "Tree is not real, but apple is real?"

"The miracles of technology," Uncle Pierce said, smiling, without any explanation. He handed the apple to Nadir, who examined it closely.

"I can eat this?" Nadir asked in amazement.

"You certainly can, but wait until after our meal," Uncle Pierce said, "so you won't be too full to enjoy the entire course."

I was still baffled by the fact that we were inside a mountain, but my senses were telling me we were outside. Even the air seemed fresh and crisp in here, but I was pretty sure it was dark outside the mountain.

"What are you hungry for?" Uncle Pierce asked, looking at each of us.

"Everything," Sammy said.

"The special of the day is fish," Uncle Pierce said. "I believe it is fresh salmon. Do you like that?"

"We like every kind of food," Nadir said. Lena nodded in agreement.

"You have salmon here?" my dad asked. "Real, fresh salmon?" I was sure his mouth was watering; salmon had always been one of his favorite foods.

"We have a river running through the mountain," Uncle Pierce said, shrugging his shoulders, as if it were no big deal.

He led us to a table and motioned for us to sit on the benches on either side of it. He placed his hand, palm down, on the table and said, "Six specials." A large round circle beneath his hand glowed a brilliant orange color.

At that moment, the table itself seemed to come alive. As I watched it shift and melt, a plate full of food appeared before each of us. Each plate had on it a nice piece of salmon, three kinds of vegetables, a small slice of flat bread, and something that looked to be a type of cheese.

"What, no silverware?" my dad asked, looking around the room. "Or do we have to get it ourselves?"

"We don't need silverware," Uncle Pierce said, reaching for his salmon.

"Wait, aren't we going to bless the Lord before we eat?" my dad asked.

Uncle Pierce quickly glanced around the room, as if my dad had said something forbidden. "Quietly, and make it short," he instructed.

My dad and I exchanged glances before we bowed our heads.

"Lord, bless us with this meal, as nourishment for our bodies, in the name of Jesus we pray. Amen," my dad said, the shortest prayer I had ever heard him pray.

My dad must have had the same hesitancy about eating salmon with his hands as I did, because we both watched Uncle Pierce as he dug into his meal and began to eat heartily. Nadir, Sammy and Lena began to eat their bread, so I did the same. I thought I could scoop the salmon into the flat bread, but Uncle Pierce was picking up his salmon and eating it with his fingers.

I broke off a small piece of the fish and popped it into my mouth. The jelly-like texture was such that I could not stand it, so I followed it immediately with a piece of the bread. The salmon looked so inviting, but it tasted like it might have been salmon flavored candy or something. The beautiful vegetables were gummy and rubbery. I wondered if this were real food or an imitation made to look like real food.

The others were eating without complaining, so I did my best with what I had. At least the bread was edible and tasted like real food.

"Help yourself to an apple from a tree," Uncle Pierce said, happily eating that odd food on his plate. My dad was eating much more slowly than he usually did, and I had an idea that this mystery fish was strange to him, too.

Lena and I went toward the tree-wall and we each picked an apple. I selected one that was bright red with narrow yellow stripes in it. As I was preparing my mouth for some odd texture to meet my teeth, I was pleasantly surprised to bite into the most wonderful-tasting apple I had ever eaten, so crisp and juicy, massaging my gums as my teeth bit into it.

Lena looked at me with pure delight on her face. "It is so very good!" she managed to say, through a mouthful of apple. I nodded in agreement as I took another bite and we returned to the table.

"This is the best apple in the world," I said, wondering how they had made it. Was it natural, or had they somehow manufactured it to make it so perfect? I was afraid to ask.

"So, Layla, what was so urgent about the message you received and decoded?" Uncle Pierce asked, as his empty plate disappeared into the table.

I looked at my dad, wondering how much to tell Uncle Pierce. He was my uncle, yes, but could I trust him with this information? I did not know anything about his life here, and what did he know about the Complex?

My dad gave me a little nod, the go-ahead to speak freely to my uncle, to tell him our secret.

"The message was from my friend, Kenrick, who lives back in the Complex, where I was living, across the world, in an area of the former United States."

Uncle Pierce's expression of amusement instantly changed to real concern. I sensed that he wanted to say something, but I continued before he could speak.

"Kenrick is a Comgen, a computer genius, and he is the one who got me over here in the first place," I explained, then decided not to reveal too much about my friend back home, or, my former home, anyway. "The message he sent was about my mother."

Uncle Pierce's mouth dropped open and I could almost see his tonsils.

"What about her?" he asked anxiously.

"Kenrick knows where she is now," I said.

The question on his mind at that moment must have been about his wife. If my mother had been found, was she with her sister? I knew he was wondering about that, because I was, too.

"Where is your mother?" he asked, lowering his voice.

"I don't know," I said. "Kenrick didn't have a chance to tell me. That's why I wanted to answer his message right away."

Lena, Nadir and Sammy were looking at me longingly, and I somehow felt ashamed or guilty that I had a chance they would never have – a chance to see my mother again.

"Did the message say anything else?" Uncle Pierce asked hopefully.

"No, just that he found her," I said, eager to get back to that computer room so I could continue my coded conversation with Kenrick.

"Are we all finished eating?" my dad asked, as he began to rise from the table. No one was touching the rest of his food, since I had made the announcement about my mom. I could tell my dad was as eager to start looking for her as I was, maybe even more so.

"You kids, finish your meals," Uncle Pierce urged, nodding his head at us as he glanced around the room. I had the sudden feeling that he didn't want to draw any attention to us, for some reason.

"Salmon is not my favorite food," I said, trying to not hurt his feelings because I didn't like fish prepared this way. I was full after eating that magnificent apple, and I was too excited to eat any more.

"We must fix food for Salwa," Lena said.

"Uncle Pierce," I said, "our friend Salwa is back in the room and we need to take some food to her."

"It is already done," he stated. "I had a meal sent to her while we were on our way here."

"How you do that?" Nadir asked.

"Technology, my young friend, technology," was the answer Uncle Pierce gave. His mind seemed to be somewhere else, and I had a feeling it was on my Aunt Moon.

"She is eating technology?" Sammy asked, confused. "What this does mean?"

"I think he means he ordered it and had it sent to her by using technology," my dad explained, as Uncle Pierce was examining a little green device he had pulled from his pocket.

"Who is this Technology person?" Lena asked.

I let out a little laugh. "Technology is not a person, but Uncle Pierce ordered the meal using some kind of technological device, and the food was sent to the room where Salwa is."

"I see," Sammy said, nodding, probably understanding it about as well as I did, which was minimal.

Sammy and Nadir finished the food that was on their plates, and when Uncle Pierce spoke into his little green device, our dishes melted into the table.

"Do you want to take a few apples with you?" Uncle Pierce asked us.

"Yes!" Lena and I exclaimed.

We all walked over to the walls and picked some apples. Sammy opened his backpack and we put most of them inside it. I saved one to carry along with me, since I knew how good they tasted, and Nadir began to eat one as we walked.

As we left the Apple Tree Room, I noticed that Uncle Pierce was not leading us in the direction of the computer room, but the opposite way down the hall. He was walking at a rather rapid pace.

"Where are we going?" I asked.

My dad shrugged as we followed Uncle Pierce. We stepped through a doorway and suddenly we were outside the mountain, standing on a balcony. The air was crisp and cool, fresh and clear.

I gazed at the most breath-taking view I had ever seen, from our high vantage point on the mountain. We could see the volcano in the distance, sitting in the midst of a beautiful mountain range. The sun was just peeking over one of the mountains, turning the clouds above it the most amazing colors of orange, pink and purple. Although my internal time clock was telling me it was evening, my sense of direction was telling me that we were looking toward the sunrise in the east.

"What time is it?" I asked.

"That is irrelevant," Uncle Pierce said curtly, still fiddling with that distracting green device.

I felt a little hurt by his dismissal of my question, and my dad must have sensed it, because he lovingly put his arm across my shoulders, holding me gently.

"This is most beautiful picture I have ever seen," Lena remarked, gazing into the distance.

"It IS picture!" Nadir said, gasping. He reached out, across the balcony railing, and tried to touch it.

"Be careful!" I said, grabbing for his arm, so he would not lose his balance and fall down the mountainside.

"How did you know?" Uncle Pierce asked, looking at Lena and Nadir suspiciously. "How could you tell it is not real?"

I looked again at the beautiful scene, trying to see what they saw, but my eyes could not comprehend that I was looking at a picture.

"Are you saying that we are not really outside on a balcony, looking at the sunrise?" I asked, astonished, as I turned toward Uncle Pierce. "But it feels and smells like we are outside!"

As I stared at the beautiful scene, the colors began to change ever so slightly, as the sun was rising above the horizon. If this were not real, then I could not trust my own eyes!

"Technology is incredible, isn't it?" Uncle Pierce said, not even answering my question. He was looking at with his little green device, and I wondered what was so interesting about it.

"What are you doing, anyway?" I asked. "What is that thing?"

Although we appeared to be alone, standing on a balcony high up on the edge of a mountain, Uncle Pierce glanced around us, as if checking for eavesdroppers. I followed his gaze, but all I could see was the magnificent view we had from this high point on the side of the mountain. I squinted my eyes, to see if I could see through the illusion, but it was too real to me. I could not see past it.

Uncle Pierce lowered his voice. "You can call your friend using this communicator," he said to me. "Your voice and your words will be scrambled so only he can understand you." He held out the device to me, and I took it tentatively.

"How can I call him?" I asked, as I examined this little green box. I could not see how to open it, or how to do anything with it. "I don't have the code to call his Wat-Com."

"You can locate him by name," Uncle Pierce said.

"What do you mean?" I asked, staring up at my uncle. "Are you saying that you have a directory of everyone who lives in the Complex?"

"The Complex?" he said, with a little shake of his head. "I don't know what you are talking about. This communicator can find people by name."

"What are you talking about?" I asked, still not understanding what he meant.

"Just try it," he said, nudging me a tiny bit. "It's one of the miracles of technology."

"Wait a minute," my dad interjected. "Miracles are not made by man, miracles are only done by our Lord and Creator, God. It might be a wonder or phenomena of technology, but nothing about anything man has made is a miracle."

"Come on, Obiad, it's just an expression," Uncle Pierce said. "Don't go all religious on me."

"It is an expression that you should not be using," my dad scolded. "By the way, I am not going 'all religious.' I love God, and that is that."

"Well, so do I, but I don't go around talking about it all the time," Uncle Pierce said.

"Maybe you should," my dad suggested. "Then you can keep it straight in your mind, the difference between what He can do and what man can do."

"And, anyway, how can I call Kenrick with this – this box?" I asked.

"Speak to it and it will respond," Uncle Pierce said

with a smile.

"This is magic box?" Sammy asked, leaning in for a closer look. "It can talk?"

"No such thing as magic," Lena said, looking at my dad for his approval.

He smiled at her, but none of their sidetracked conversation was helping me figure out how to be able to contact Kenrick!

"Just speak to it," Uncle Pierce said. "Go ahead, see what happens."

"Little green box, please call my friend, Kenrick," I said, speaking to the box.

"No match found," a voice from the box said.

"Wow, that voice sounds exactly like your voice!" Nadir said, bending down to take a closer look at the strange green device.

Uncle Pierce just smiled at us.

"So, it didn't work," I said, turning it over in my hand, to find the hidden way in or out of it.

"We must hurry," Uncle Pierce said, suddenly with a sense of urgency.

"So, what should I do now?" I asked. "Can't we just go back to the computer so I can send him a coded message? That would be much easier."

"And that would also attract the attention of everyone here at Mountain Veil," Uncle Pierce said. "Layla, use his other name," he suggested.

"What other name?" I asked, searching my memory for any other name he might be using, and at the same time wondering why Uncle Pierce would think Kenrick had another name. I was beginning to get suspicious of Uncle Pierce. How could he know so much about Kenrick, when until earlier today – or was it yesterday? – Uncle Pierce did not even know my dad and I were still alive. Or perhaps he didn't know and he was just guessing.

I tried to picture Kenrick at the Complex – a world away and lifetimes away from my current situation. He could be at any of his workstations, or using any computer in his pod or anywhere in the entire Complex, since he controlled all of them. Even when he was being watched, none of the adults could understand what he was doing on the computers, so he was quite free in that respect. However, others could possibly intercept an incoming signal, even if they were not able to decode it, since I wasn't there to do my job. They would know a signal had come from somewhere. I had assumed this would be a bad thing, but actually, the ones in charge of the Complex might be helped if they discovered they didn't rule the entire civilized world.

A quick memory of Kenrick with Big Hawk and Hiding Cathy, as we were together in Kenrick's pod flashed through my mind, and, although I was completely satisfied living a new life with my dad, I felt a pang in my heart; I did miss my friends. They had been like family to me in recent years, and I had not had time to even think about them since meeting up with my dad. I had no doubt that Kenrick and Big Hawk had made it back to the Complex without any trouble, but I wondered what they were doing now? At least Kenrick knew that I was okay – and he knew I was in a civilization that used technology.

"Water Closet Free Zone!" I suddenly shouted, recalling that one spot in Kenrick's pod where we could not be monitored, either by video, audio, or through our personal devices.

The others looked at me as if I had just gone completely crazy. Uncle Pierce had a big question mark on his forehead, and Nadir, Lena and Sammy just stared at me with their eyes bugging out of their heads.

The device in my hand began to feel warm, then it began to vibrate. I was so startled, I nearly dropped it, and then, as if the most natural thing in the world, Kenrick began to talk to me.

"Layla, it's so good to hear from you," he said. His conversation seemed to be a bit guarded, so I chose my words carefully.

"Hi, Kenrick, it's good to hear your voice."

I could barely hold my tongue from asking about my mom, but I knew I had to wait until he gave me the go-ahead.

"Do you want to meet where we last parted?" he asked casually.

Suddenly I began to panic. Was I going to be forced to go back to the Complex? What about my dad? Could he go with me? Kenrick knew where my mom was, but he did not know I had found my dad! I could not bear to part from him. No, we had to go together to find my mother.

"I am not near there," I answered slowly and deliberately.

"I can locate you," he suggested. I knew he would be able to pinpoint our location within a matter of seconds, if he had not already.

My mind was racing. I was not going to leave my dad, that was for sure, and I knew Uncle Pierce would want to go with us as well. Another scene flashed in my mind: Mom and Aunt Moon were laughing, doubling over with laughter, when we were at the Mall Quadrant, just before Uncle Pierce had called Aunt Moon in a panic, and told us to meet him on the airplane. That had been just before our entire world was turned upside down.

Plus, wherever I was going, my new friends had to go also. I was not about to leave them here, in this strange place, while I went clear across to the other side of the world, back to a life where I would most surely be punished, and perhaps even jailed, separated from my dad… and so how could I take them with me?

But wait, I was forgetting about the power of Kenrick. He had the authority to clear my absence and even erase it, making it seem like I had never left the Complex; or that I had left, with permission. Even so, I could not go back to that sterile, structured substitute for a life, not after finding my dad and experiencing a life filled with family and love!

The Complex was not our destination. Our destination had to be the place where my mother was living.

CHAPTER 2

"We are inside a mountain," I said quickly, into the green communication device.

Uncle Pierce grabbed it from me and began to talk to Kenrick. "Forty-five by twenty north and west of here, how soon can you meet us there? We have a landing strip and six people," he said quickly. He was at least as anxious as I was to get some answers!

He and Kenrick worked out a schedule which would give us just a few minutes to get back to our rooms to get our things together and head to the landing strip. As Uncle Pierce parted from us to gather his own supplies, I turned to my dad.

"Wait! We are seven people!" I exclaimed. "He didn't count Salwa!"

"Maybe your uncle is not planning to go," Nadir suggested.

"He is going," my dad and I said at the same time. We looked at each other and laughed as we arrived at our room.

"We will get our backpacks and meet you back here, pronto," my dad said, as we entered our room.

"What is this, pronto?" Lena asked, shaking her head at me.

"That is slang for right away, immediately, in just a minute," I explained, going in to check on Salwa, who was still asleep in the bedroom.

Lena brought Salwa's dinner, which was on a tray near the door, and she placed it on a small table beside the bed. Lena touched her gently and said something quietly in their language as Salwa began to stretch. I ran into the bathroom to brush my teeth while I had the opportunity.

When I came out of the bathroom, they were both sitting on the bed, looking at me.

"We cannot go with you," Lena announced. "Salwa not feeling good, and I must to stay with her, here."

"We can't leave you here!" I protested. "Maybe Sammy can carry her again, like he did before."

Salwa said something that I didn't understand. I looked from one to the other, to get an explanation.

"She feeling very hot," Lena said, gently stroking Salwa's head. Salwa put her head on the pillow and closed her eyes.

"Well, then, we should all stay here until you get better," I said. "I am sure they have medicine here. Remember how they fixed my dad's hand, back at that other place? We are not in that big of a hurry. We can wait for you to get better."

As if on cue, my dad, Nadir and Sammy rushed into our main room. I could see them from where I was standing in the bedroom.

"We are ready to go," Nadir said, impatiently looking around the room.

"We are in here," I called, and my dad peeked his head into the room.

"Are you ready?" he asked.

"Salwa doesn't feel well, and she might have a fever," I said, my hopes slowly sinking. "We can't leave her here alone, and she can't come with us in this condition."

"I am to stay with her," Lena insisted, looking over Salwa like a mother with her child.

"No, you go," Sammy urged, pushing passed my dad and Nadir to get close to the bedroom. "I stay with Salwa. I stay here and I take care of her."

"I cannot leave her, my sister," Lena argued.

"Lena, she is in good hands with Sammy," Nadir said. "You come with us."

"I cannot," Lena said, shaking her head. "She need me to stay with her."

"We need you to come with us," Nadir insisted, and I felt he meant to say '*I* need you.' I felt a tiny bit jealous, but, actually, they were family, and I understood that he really did need her. He held his hand out to her.

She looked at his hand, then back at Salwa, undecided. Suddenly Uncle Pierce dashed into the living quarters, frantically scanning the rooms until he saw us in the bedroom. From his eyes, I caught a sense of urgency.

"We are ready, but two of our young people will have to stay here," my dad informed him. "Layla, Lena, Nadir, let's go."

Sammy stayed firmly planted by Salwa as the rest of us began to move. Uncle Pierce reached into his pack and tossed something to Sammy. I grabbed my backpack and saw Sammy examining the small item.

"We can keep in touch with these," Uncle Pierce told him, ushering the group out of the room. He led us down the long hallway and put his hand up to the wall, in a space where I could see nothing but wall. All of a sudden, the wall appeared to dissolve and, at Uncle Pierce's silent shove, we crowded into a small room that

I perceived to be an elevator; yet it had no buttons. The wall reappeared, enclosing us, and we instantly began what felt to me like a free-fall. My head seemed to stay at the level where we had just been, while my body was going down, faster than I could imagine. I felt dizzy, sick to my stomach, then we were absorbed by a feeling of being cushioned, and the wall on the other side of the room dissolved.

As we exited the dropping box that had just landed softly, and I tried to get my legs to function normally, we found ourselves inside a huge cave.

"I know you are curious, but we are really in a hurry," Uncle Pierce said, before I could even ask him about it. "We are at the base of Mountain Veil, but many layers above the lowest layer, and we are in a top-secret area. Get into that vehicle, quickly."

He pointed to something that looked like a bullet, one of those old-fashioned kind they used way back in one of the previous centuries. It was gold, rounded, long and narrow, and it had a sharp point on one end and was flat on the other end. As we approached it, a portion of the side dissolved to let us climb into it. From the inside, we could see through the gold to the outside, giving a one-way mirror effect. We were tightly compacted into the vehicle, and I briefly thought that if Sammy and Salwa had been with us, we would not have been able to fit.

Uncle Pierce was the last to enter. He had something in his hand, similar to the green communicator we had used to contact Kenrick, but this one was gold, perfectly matching the vehicle. He spoke into it and the side of the vehicle that had dissolved suddenly was back on again.

Then we began to move like a bullet that had been shot out of a cannon, zooming across the floor – or were we even touching the floor? I didn't think so, we were shooting through the cave area, and I instinctively closed my eyes right before the impact with the wall of the cave. Only there was no impact. When I opened my eyes again, we were rocketing across the desert, a short distance above the sagebrush and cactuses. The scenery was a blur, and I realized it actually was very early morning, not late evening like my senses were telling me, with the desert colors condensed to darks and lights.

As we zipped straight toward our destination, I began to feel sick to my stomach. All this high-speed movement, first dropping down in the mountain and now whizzing across the landscape, was not good for my inward parts, my tummy nor my head. I closed my eyes for a few seconds, but that made it worse, like falling off a cliff in the dark. When I dared to peek, the vehicle was beginning to slow, as we reached the landing strip.

Uncle Pierce guided the bullet vehicle to one side of the strip, and as it was hovering just above the ground, we climbed out of it. The ground seemed to be moving under my wobbly legs, making me wonder if a tremor was shaking the earth; but, no, it was just that after moving so fast, my body didn't know what to do with a ground beneath me that was standing still!

"I don't see him here," Uncle Pierce said, stating the obvious as we looked around, down the landing strip and in the air. He then did the strangest thing. Using his remote device, he controlled the bullet vehicle, turning it on its nose, so the point was standing on the ground. He quietly said, "Go," and the vehicle shot –

like a bullet – right into the ground. It went beneath ground level, and sand quickly covered it. I stared at the spot, blinking my eyes, thinking about how it was right there but we could no longer see it.

"He IS here!" I suddenly shouted.

The others looked at me as if I had lost all of my bananas, as I began to walk down the landing strip and the plane came into sight, smack dab in front of me. I nearly bumped into it, the camouflaged/invisible plane. Kenrick opened a door and came down the stairway. I ran over to give him a hug before I could think about it. He, clearly embarrassed, barely hugged me back.

"Where did you come from?" Uncle Pierce asked, looking at the newly visible plane right in front of us.

"It's a cammy plane," Kenrick said, not bothering with any other explanation. "Come on, let's get going." He also was not bothering with any introductions, nor did he seem surprised that I was here with four other people, as he turned around and boarded the plane.

"That is my good friend, Kenrick," I said to my dad, Uncle Pierce, Nadir and Lena. "He is the one who got me here; well, not here, to this place, but here, to this side of the world."

"It's nice to meet you, Kenrick," my dad said politely, even though Kenrick was already inside the plane.

"We don't have much time," Kenrick said quickly, motioning for us to hurry and get on the plane.

The men stepped aside and let Lena and me climb the steps first. Nadir followed, with my dad and Uncle Pierce right behind him.

"I am going to close the door now," Kenrick announced, stepping over near the door. He had to yell, because the engines were beginning to roar.

"Wait!" I shouted. "I left my backpack in the… what do you call it? The bullet-car!" I went running out through the door and down the steps before anyone could stop me, only to remember that Uncle Pierce had embedded the vehicle deep in the desert sand. When I turned around, Uncle Pierce had jumped out of the plane, the door was closing, and the plane was already moving down the runway.

"Wait!" I shouted again, starting to run after the plane and feeling so foolish, because, how important was the backpack, anyway? The computer was inside it, but the backpack was buried in the bullet-vehicle. My dad and my friends were taking off in the plane, and Uncle Pierce and I were left standing near the runway.

"What is so important about your backpack?" Uncle Pierce yelled, over the sound of the jet engines.

"They can't leave us!" I insisted.

"They just did!" Uncle Pierce said, as we watched the plane disappear into the clouds.

CHAPTER 3

"What are we going to do?" I asked frantically. "How are we going to catch them?" I stared hard at the clouds, willing the plane to turn around and bring my dad back to me. I felt tears begin to sting my eyes. I could not lose my dad again, not now!

Uncle Pierce took the green device out of his pocket and I heard a strange whirring behind me. The bullet-vehicle was unscrewing itself from the ground, lifting up, and it came to hover beside us. The side dissolved.

"Get in," Uncle Pierce said loudly, and he followed me as I climbed in and sat down. "Put on that safety belt," he said.

I did as he instructed. As soon as the side of the vehicle had reappeared, we were moving fast, this time, up into the sky, in the same direction as the plane had gone.

"I will attempt to lock onto the plane's coordinates, so we can follow it," Uncle Pierce said. The inside of the vehicle was surprisingly quiet, so he could speak using his normal voice.

"I have a few questions I have been wanting to ask you," I said. Now that we were on track, I did not need to panic, and we were alone, I had questions like, what did he know about the Complex? Why didn't he just fly us all the way to where Kenrick was, using this vehicle? Why did I have the feeling that the inside of that mountain city was a military base, preparing for a war? And, most importantly, was he absolutely positive that we could catch up with Kenrick so I could be reunited with my dad?

"No time for chit-chat now," he said, looking at some sort of holographic scope. "Here, hold that lever, and don't let it move to the left or right." He pointed to a lever in front of me that must have appeared out of nowhere, because it had not been there just a moment ago.

I grabbed it with both hands, but it didn't seem to be going anywhere.

"Hold on tight," he said, as we were lifted higher and higher into the clouds.

The lever began to vibrate, so I gripped it as tightly as I could. Now I was frightened. I could not see a thing, only the whiteness of the clouds, and I had this strange feeling that we, moving at this tremendous speed, were going to crash into the back of the plane. I closed my eyes, not wanting to see the impact, as my heart pounded, knowing we would hit it any second.

We did not hit. We were suddenly above the clouds, under the most beautiful blue sky I had ever seen. My mind was telling me that we were still moving very fast, but my eyes could not confirm it. We seemed to be just floating up in the air.

"Where is the plane?" I asked, looking ahead of us, scanning the skies.

Uncle Pierce did not answer me. He was examining the little green device and the hologram at the same time, looking back and forth, from one to the other, and then out the windows, to the front and to the side.

"You are my copilot," he said, not taking his eyes off of what he was doing. "Make sure you have a good hold on that lever."

I was holding the lever as if it were the only thing

keeping us in the air. "Okay," I said, deciding this was not the time for conversation. I needed to listen to his directions, and we could talk about other things later.

The lever wanted to drift off to the left, so I had to use a little muscle to keep it in the middle, right where it was. The only thing I knew about being a copilot was that the pilot was in charge, and I was to do whatever he told me to do. Holding the lever steady was beginning to take my full concentration. I did not want to ask what might happen if I could not hold it. We were really high up in the air, and, worst case scenario, we could begin to descend very quickly, and that could not end well for us. No, I didn't want to know about that. I just held on to the lever with all of my might.

We kept going, and, with a blanket of clouds beneath us, I wondered if we had passed the cammy plane; after all, it was extremely difficult to see, especially when it was in the air, and we were moving fast. After all, we were in a bullet, one of the most aerodynamic shapes, and we were shooting through the sky.

"Hold on!" Uncle Pierce said, loudly and firmly.

All of a sudden, we were bursting through the clouds and we zipped by a mountain peak, just off to our right.

"Where are we?" I asked, trying my best to keep my voice steady.

Uncle Pierce just kept flying the bullet vehicle, and I kept holding the lever, doing my best to keep it from moving. Now it was pulling hard to the right, and I was using all my strength to keep it from going anywhere.

We dropped in altitude, quite a long distance. My ears popped and my head felt like it was floating way up where we had just been. I felt dizzy, and I was afraid

I was going to lose consciousness; but suddenly we were zipping along the desert again, and the sun was just rising again.

Uncle Pierce slowed the vehicle, and we were cruising along at a much slower pace than we had been going.

"How did we get back here?" I asked. "Did we break the sound barrier? Why is the sun coming up again?" I felt as if I were in some weird dream, one that I had just had and was destined to have again and again. "Where is the plane? Where is my dad? We have to find him! Where is he? Did the plane land somewhere around here? I can't lose my dad again!"

I examined the landscape, trying to see the invisible plane, but I was pretty sure it was not there. I knew it was not in sight, thus, an invisible plane; but I could feel that it was not anywhere in the vicinity. Our vehicle came to a stop.

"Patience, my dear Layla, patience," Uncle Pierce said, as he rubbed his hand over the green communicator device and the sides of the bullet vehicle dissolved. He climbed out of the vehicle, extended himself to his full height, and took in the scenery. If I hadn't known exactly what we were doing, I might have thought he was merely sightseeing in a beautiful area. He looked to the left and to the right, and I noticed that something caught his interest.

I scrambled out of the vehicle as quickly as I could, this time, remembering to grab my backpack, and I slung it over my shoulder as I was looking in the same direction where Uncle Pierce was looking. That was when I realized that we were not in the same desert where the landing strip was. In the distance, toward where the sun was rising in the east, was a long row of hills. Only these were not like any hills I had ever seen; these hills were all flat on the top, as if they had at one time been normal hills with rounded tops and someone had come with a giant knife and sliced off the tops, to make them all the same height and perfectly flat. I couldn't see the details of the hills, if they had trees or ridges, because of the angle of the sun, but I was sure these were not the same hills I had crossed with my dad and my friends. At this realization, I was somewhat relieved, because I did not want to be back where we had started; so at least we were getting somewhere.

"Where are we?" I asked, looking up at Uncle Pierce.

"I am not entirely sure," was his unsatisfactory answer. He was still looking, searching for something, but he was distracted. He began looking from his green device and out to the desert, one to the other. Perhaps he was attempting to discern our location. Whatever he was doing, he was not communicating it with me.

As the sun was rising, colors slowly to appear around us. We were in an extremely beautiful place. In this area, the plant life consisted of mostly cactus of several varieties. I was fascinated by one that was near us that had flat, paddle-like branches with long needles sticking out of it. Also, there were clumps of grass that had very long blades, which seemed oddly out of habitat. I was staring at one of the clumps when I began to hear something.

"Did you hear that?" I whispered loudly to Uncle Pierce.

"Hear what?" he asked, not even whispering, and only partially paying attention to me.

"Shhh!" I said, and I slowly began to move in the direction of the sound, which was to the west of us.

Yet, then the sound seemed to be coming from another direction, sort of to the south of us, but it was growing a bit louder.

"I don't hear anything," Uncle Pierce said, still focusing on his green device. He had not moved from his original spot, and he didn't seem to notice that I was moving.

"I hear it," I said, still walking slowly, trying to figure out what kind of sound it was. Could it be a buzzing or a humming? Perhaps a colony of giant hornets was barely beyond my sight? Whatever it was, I could feel the buzzing, not just in my ears and in my head, but in my whole body, a vibration. Was it coming from inside of me? That was not very likely. This was more like the entire earth was beginning to rumble.

"Layla!" Uncle Pierce called to me, from a great distance.

I turned to him and I became aware that I had walked quite a long ways, drawn to the buzzing sound, now so prominent that I felt like a swarm of bees was circling my head.

"What are you doing?" Uncle Pierce began running toward me, and as he drew near to me, I saw a look of panic in his eyes. "I can't lose you," he said frantically, when he caught up to me. I noticed that he was not even out of breath, letting me know that he must have been in pretty good shape.

"I hear something over there," I said, pointing, "like a buzzing sound. I can feel it buzzing inside of me."

"I'm not sure we should go there," Uncle Pierce said, causing me to stop in my tracks. Something about the tone of his voice made feel afraid.

"Why not?" I asked tentatively, still looking in that direction. Something was odd, a very curious matter, to the west of us.

"I think something happened to the plane," he said, with more than just a little bit of worry in his voice.

"Why do you think that?" I asked, turning to look at him. I could not lose my dad again! "No, nothing happened to it! Kenrick knows what he is doing, and he would not let anything happen to it!" I began shaking my head so hard, I made myself dizzy.

"We were tracking the plane, all the way to this point," he said, "so I landed us here, and the plane is not here. It has completely disappeared from my tracking scope."

"Oh, you don't know Kenrick," I said, relieved. "He is just cloaking it so they can't find it."

"They?" he asked. "Who are 'they'?"

"The leaders at the Complex," I explained, again looking to the west, and trying to figure out what seemed so odd about this picture of the desert. "We must be in the range of where they can track us."

My statement suddenly made me feel very disturbed. What if they were tracking us? They could have a legion out here pronto, to capture us and take us back to the Complex. I glanced at our surroundings, but still, no one else was in sight.

Uncle Pierce was looking at me in a strange way, almost like he did not believe me.

"The Complex?" he asked, as if this were the first time I had mentioned it, and it were a new concept to him.

"Yes, the Complex, where I have been living for the last nine years," I said, wondering if he had been listening to me at all since we found him at Mountain Veil. "If they are tracking us, they will know exactly where we are."

"Well, of course, that would be the reason for tracking," he said, smiling at me. He did not seem to be worried now. "They can't track the bullet-jetcar. It has a built in scrambler so it can't be tracked. Besides, since it's so small and so fast, it can't even be captured on sight recognition satellites."

He turned around so he was facing the bullet-jetcar, as he called it, and he moved his hand over the green communicator device. I looked back to see the bullet-jetcar far in the distance, and the sun was shining right in my eyes. I blocked the sunlight with my hand just in time to see the bullet-jetcar shoot into the sand, as it had before. Now I was confident that it was completely hidden… but how would Kenrick find us?

Uncle Pierce must have been reading my mind, because he said, "I tried to contact your friend with my communicator, but I have not received a response."

I turned away from the rising sun and suddenly realized what was so odd ahead of us. The landscape was too bright! Another sun could not be rising in the west, but the brightness of the glowing ground was immense.

"What is that?" I asked, not really expecting Uncle Pierce to know, but simply needing to ask the question.

We stood there for a moment as my mind raced, expecting something exceedingly brilliant to rise out of the ground in the distance any second; if not a miniature planet, perhaps a spaceship?

Uncle Pierce began to walk slowly toward the light, his eyes fixed upon it, pulled by its intensity. As I moved along with him, not letting the light control me, but looking back and forth from it to my uncle, I was aware that the buzzing was growing louder, vibrating inside my heart. The brightness became too bright, mirroring the brightness of the sun, and we shielded our eyes. Uncle Pierce pulled out his green device and looked directly at it while I focused on him. Besides the buzzing, I could now feel an intense heat coming from the light, and I started to sweat. This was not simply the heat of the desert, this heat was coming from the opposite direction as the sun.

In the near distance, like a mirage, a group of trees and a small pool of water appeared. I blinked, sure that I was imagining it, but as we grew closer, I could see that the trees were casting shadows toward us. Before we knew it, we were in the shade of the trees, yet still in the sunlight that was shining behind us. A movement in a small bush beside us just about scared me to death, and a little rabbit skittered across the sand to another bush farther away from us.

"Who are you?" a young voice out of nowhere asked, startling me even further. I jumped higher than I ever thought possible. If my heart were not being pumped by the buzzing inside of me, it might have stopped beating altogether.

CHAPTER 4

"Who are you?" Uncle Pierce asked, as we searched for the source of the voice. My eyes were still adjusting to looking in shadows after all that brightness burned into them, so when I saw a movement just out of the corner of my eye, at first I thought it was my imagination. Yet, as I turned to face the illusion, there he stood, a boy about eight or nine years old, appearing in my sight. He had dark, curly hair and his brown eyes had a glint of mischief in them. He was dressed in red clothing – a red shirt, red pants, and red shoes.

"I asked you first," he said defiantly, crossing his hands across his chest.

"Where did you come from?" Uncle Pierce asked.

"That's what I want to know," the boy said. "You don't live here. So, where do you live? How did you get here?"

"Where are we?" I asked.

"Do you guys always answer a question with another question?" the boy asked, as he looked from Uncle Pierce to me and back.

"Are there other people here?" I wondered, looking around for any other people who might be materializing near us.

"Don't you know anything?" the boy asked.

"We don't know anything about this place," Uncle Pierce said.

"What place do you know about?" the boy said, looking at us curiously. "Did you come from another planet, in outer space?"

"No," I laughed, "but we don't know exactly where we are."

"You are a silly girl!" the boy shouted. "I thought girls were supposed to be smart, and you don't even know where you are? You are right here, of course! Where else would you be?"

"We came from the other side of the earth," Uncle Pierce said, his way of explaining.

"That is impossible!" the boy said. "Nobody lives on the other side of the earth!"

"Actually, quite a few people live there," Uncle Pierce said calmly.

"Oh, do you really expect me to believe that?" the boy asked, then his eyes grew wide as he began to inspect us closely. "I know who you are! You are the Enemy! You came to spy on us, and you are going to capture all of us and lock us up! Well, you can't catch me! Especially, no girl can catch me!"

With that, the boy took off in a sprint. What could we do? We had to follow him, so Uncle Pierce and I started running.

"Wait!" I called, my legs already growing tired. I had worked them more in the last week than I had my entire life, and my muscles were telling me so.

"We are not the Enemy!" Uncle Pierce shouted, as he was closing in on the boy. "We are looking for my wife!"

The boy and I stopped running at the same time. I think we were both in shock to hear that confession. I thought we were looking for my dad first, and then for my mother. The boy turned to look at Uncle Pierce.

"Are you my dad?" the boy asked, examining my uncle closely.

CHAPTER 5

"How can I be your dad?" Uncle Pierce asked, as he caught up to the boy. I arrived about a half minute later, panting, trying to catch my breath. Uncle Pierce touched the boy's shoulder. "I have never seen you before."

"And I have never seen my dad before," the boy said, standing up tall, so he could look my uncle in the eye. "That is why you might be my dad."

"What is your name, anyway?" I asked.

"I asked you first," the boy said, looking me straight in the eye. His eyes were somewhat familiar, but I couldn't quite place where I had seen such eyes before.

"My name is Layla," I said.

The boy's eyes just about popped out of his head as he stared at me. "Layla?" he repeated, looking me up and down. "You are Layla?"

"Yes…" I said, wondering what that was all about.

"You are Layla?" he asked again. He walked around me, presumably to see if I were a real person or just a ghost.

"She is Layla," Uncle Pierce confirmed.

"Are you Layla's dad?" the boy asked, looking up at Uncle Pierce.

"No, I am her uncle," he said. "So, you have not told us your name."

"I have to go and get my mom," the boy said, without answering the question. "You have to come with me! I have to tell her! Follow me! Oh, no, I hope it is not too late!"

He took off running, so we had no choice but to run

after him. He led us away from the oasis, through the desert. He began to slow down as we approached an incline.

"We are going to go in through here," the boy said, "and please don't tell my mom I came up here, because we are not allowed."

"They why did you come here" I asked, following him down on the rock steps, "if you are not allowed?"

"Oh, I always come up here," he said, "so I can get away from everyone for awhile."

"Wait!" I said. "What do you mean, 'everyone'? Are there very many people here?"

"Yeah, thousands," he said nonchalantly.

"Are you sure?" Uncle Pierce said. "Thousands of people live around here?"

"Not *around* here," the boy said, "but right here, in our city."

"You have a city here?" I asked, glancing at the bare desert around us. "I don't see a city."

"Well, not right here in this exact spot where we are standing, of course, but down there," he said, pointing. "We don't want the Enemy to see us, because they will come and take over the city and capture all of us and take us away and lock us up forever."

I took another step down to where the boy was pointing, with Uncle Pierce following closely behind me. I was taken aback by the picturesque sight that lay ahead of us, and I gasped. We were looking into a canyon of sorts, as we stood at the upper rim, down at one end. Across from us, on the other rim of the canyon, was the source of the brightness. The other side was the exact same height as the rim where we were standing. It was coated in gold, clear across that whole top half of that side of the canyon, from one end to the other, and the sun was reflecting off of it. Below the enormous band of gold that stretched across the canyon wall were four rows of windows and below those windows, down at the bottom of the canyon wall, were larger windows with doors in between them, like a line of stores.

The windows were bordered with ornate trim, and behind one window was women's clothing, behind another was men's clothing, behind a third window were household items; each window held a beautiful display of goods. We were looking down into a city street, a downtown area that looked to be straight out of the Time Before, only much more glamorous and sparkling clean. The scene was almost too perfect, like it was a movie set. I had seen pictures and films of how people had created fake towns of all eras so they could make movies set in different time periods, and this place was strangely like that, except for the abundance of people.

People were down there everywhere: going in and out of the doors, walking up and down the lane between the two walls of the canyon, criss-crossing from one side to the other. They were talking, laughing, running, and they seemed to be having a great time, doing whatever they were doing. Although we were quite a distance above them, I immediately noticed something odd about them. From where we stood, I could see that they were all dressed in red. Red masses were flowing around in the bottom of this canyon. I had never seen so many people in my entire life.

"Why is everyone dressed in red?" I asked, watching the bustle of activity so far beneath us. "Did you get all your clothes on special or something? Or are you part of some weird religion that only wears red?"

"Don't you know anything?" the boy asked. "We have to wear red today because of the celebration. Everybody has to wear red. Oh, you guys have to change your clothes, so you won't get in trouble for being out of compliance."

"What are you celebrating?" Uncle Pierce asked. I was wondering the same thing.

"You guys really don't know anything!" the boy said. "Today is our Day of Celebration! Come on, we have to sneak through the palace, and then I can find you some red clothes to change into. We have to get there before the wedding starts." He started to climb down the stone steps, which wound around a huge rock, out of sight.

"What?" I asked, as I hurried to follow him. "Did you say we have to sneak through a palace?"

"Really, did you say we have to sneak through a palace?" Uncle Pierce repeated, as he nearly stepped on my heel.

"Yep, it's right underneath us," the boy said. "I always do it. That's the only way to get up here. This whole side is the palace, well, the whole top part, anyway."

"Can't you just introduce us, so we don't have to sneak in through the palace?" I asked. Then I thought about how hard it might be for someone back at the Complex to try to introduce strangers to the rest of the population there, and I realized how ridiculous my question was. But still, it looked like the people here were having fun. Yet, I knew looks could be deceiving. An outsider could have mistaken our mere existence at the Complex for a fun life, if he just saw us from a distance.

"And you mentioned a wedding?" Uncle Pierce asked, as we continued to follow the boy, who still had not told us his name.

"I am not about to get myself in trouble," he said. "I would really be in for it if they knew I have been sneaking through the palace. I would never be able to come up here again if they found out about it."

As we rounded the corner, we came to an enormous door. The boy put his hand on the large handle and turned to us.

"Be quiet, and follow me. The palace should be empty, but every single person is not always exactly where he should be." He turned and gave me a knowing look, although I had no idea what he was implying. "Someone might be inside. If you just follow me, we can sneak by anybody."

He pulled the door handle with both hands, and the door opened toward us. We followed him into a dark hallway, down another stairway, around several corners, until we got to another door. He opened it just a crack and peeked through before opening it all the way.

"Just be quiet, walk quickly, and stay close to me," he instructed.

We entered a large hallway with a very high ceiling. The walls were painted a bright yellow color with a blue flower border decoration at the top. The hallway was so long, I couldn't tell how far it went. Doorways were on both sides of the hallway, all the way down. An endless fancy rug, beautiful and colorful, made long stripes from us to the other end.

The boy began to walk swiftly, his head bobbing back and forth as he looked into the rooms to our left and right as we passed them. I tried to get a glimpse into the rooms, which appeared to be quite sizeable and beautifully decorated, with fancy lighting and elaborate draperies, but we were moving so quickly, I didn't have a chance to get a good look. After we had passed about ten rooms, I realized that the rooms to our right had windows, but the ones on our left had no windows, and were much smaller and darker inside than the rooms on the right. We were inside the canyon wall, after all, but the place was so stunning and so rich, I felt that we were actually inside a real palace. I paused as we passed an extremely large room, to get a better look at the gold trim around the windows, the intricate and amazing murals painted on the wall, and the elegant furniture inside the room, and Uncle Pierce crashed into me. We tumbled to the floor, although we did not really make much noise in our fall.

"Shhh! What are you doing?" the boy whispered, trotting back to help us to our feet. "We have to get out of here."

He led us to a doorway to the right side of the hall, stopped, leaned to peek inside, then he motioned for us to follow him into the room. We entered the giant room and I took in its splendor. The draperies were a deep, rich, red color, matching the chairs and the trim around the top of the room. The entire room was accented with gold and diamonds. A beautiful golden table sat next to a ceiling-to-floor gold-framed mirror, and beside it was a large door. When the boy went over to the door and began to push it sideways, I realized it was actually two doors. The one he pushed slid right behind the other one, revealing a closet full of clothing of every color of the rainbow.

"Do you have a different color for every kind of celebration day?" I asked, impressed by this wonderful wardrobe.

"Be quiet!" the boy whispered loudly. He grabbed several red garments and tossed them to me. "Put those on. You can hide your stuff in here, in the back."

I was too embarrassed to change in front of these two males. Even though I knew Uncle Pierce, I had never changed my clothes in front of him, and I didn't know the little boy at all.

"Where can I change?" I asked, my voice barely a whisper.

He stared at me with a look of confusion, not understanding what I said. I was about to repeat my question more loudly when I heard voices coming from the hallway.

"He must be around here somewhere," a male voice said.

"No, I am sure he is just lost in the crowd," a female voice said angrily. "You know he can't stay away from food for more than a minute, and they are about to start serving."

"I saw him coming this way," the man insisted.

The boy pushed Uncle Pierce and me into the closet, back behind the clothes, just as the couple entered the room. My heart was pounding so hard, I was sure they were going to hear it, as we scrunched down in the closet, slowly inching backwards, further and further toward the back.

"He is not in here," the lady said.

"Hey!" the man said. "I didn't leave that door open!"

As the footsteps drew near to us, I held my breath, watching two pairs of red pants moving closer and closer to us. I knew the time had come when we would have to surrender to these unknown people.

CHAPTER 6

I heard a faint click behind me and as I tried to press against the closet wall, I fell backwards in the dark. I felt a tap on my shoulder that nudged me, and I kept scooting until I could turn myself around and begin to crawl, following whoever was right in front of me. I felt that we were inside a tunnel, and I recalled reading about castles and mansions and palaces of the Time Before that had all kinds of secret corridors and hidden rooms. I looked back toward the closet, but the boy must have closed the concealed door, because I could no longer see the light coming from the room.

All of a sudden, I was falling – no, I was sliding, down-down-down, on a curving slide, and I shifted my limbs so they were not under me, and I was sliding down, in the darkness, on my bottom. I kept going for such a long time, I was afraid that I would fall off the end of the slide, since the momentum was so great. My fears turned out to be a wasted fear, because near the end, the slope leveled off, and I came to a stop. A very dim light began to grow a wee bit brighter, and I could see the silhouettes of Uncle Pierce and the boy standing near the slide.

"Are you okay?" Uncle Pierce asked me, in a whisper.

"I think so," I answered, unable to find anything out of whack.

"Do you still have the red clothes?" the boy asked. He was not whispering now.

"No," I said, "they must have stayed behind when we came down the big slide."

"I told you to put them on," he said, using a little

43

boy argumentative voice. I had heard this tone of voice in old movies I had watched back at the Complex, but this was my first time hearing a real person using it.

"Excuse me, but I did not have an opportunity to put them on before you pushed me into the closet."

"Now you are really in for it," he said. "Everyone has to wear red on Celebration Day. It's the rule, and everybody has to follow it."

"Or what?" I asked. I was not sure why it was so easy to try to start an argument with him.

"Or you are really going to get in trouble," he said, as if that explained it all.

"Oh, yeah, how can we get in trouble? We don't even live here!"

"Stop it, you two," Uncle Pierce said. "If I didn't know better, I would think you were arguing like brother and sister."

"We are!" the boy said.

"I'm sorry, Uncle Pierce," I said. "We don't have to. I mean, I don't know what came over me."

"But we are!" the boy said.

"I am giving up," I said, putting up my hands in surrender. "We don't have to argue."

"We just need to talk to the person in charge," Uncle Pierce said. "Where can we find him?"

"Well…" the boy said slowly. "Which one?"

"Which one what?" Uncle Pierce asked.

"Which person in charge do you want to talk to?" the boy said evasively.

"Does it matter?" I asked. "How many people are in

charge, anyway?"

"Well…" the boy said again, "there's the Queen. She is actually the main one in charge."

"The Queen?" I asked. "You have a queen?"

"She's not my queen!" the boy sputtered.

"Who else is in charge?" Uncle Pierce said.

"Well, there are the two princes," the boy said reluctantly, "and then there is my mom. She is really the one who is in charge of me."

"Take us to the Queen," Uncle Pierce instructed.

"No, you can't get in to see the Queen, especially right before the wedding."

"Is the Queen getting married?" I asked, curious about a wedding. I could not ever remember attending a wedding, and they certainly never had any at the Complex.

"No, are you kidding?" the boy asked with a laugh. "The Queen can never get married. She is too old!"

"So, take us the princes," Uncle Pierce said, the next logical step.

"I don't think they will be happy," the boy said. "At least one of them will be really mad at us, if he knows we just were in his quarters."

"How can he know that?" I asked, suddenly beginning to panic.

"That was him, upstairs," the boy said.

"We were hiding in the closet of the Prince?" Uncle Pierce asked. I detected a note of anxiety in his voice.

"He has lots of closets!" the boy said. "I did not know he was going to come to that one just now."

"Why do I feel like you are not telling us the whole story?" I asked. I knew there had to be more to it, even though I wanted more than anything to get out of this dark and creepy place.

"They were looking for me," the boy quietly confessed.

"Do they know about the secret slide?" I asked. "Can they follow us down here?"

"I am sure the prince knows about it, but he doesn't know that I know about it," the boy said.

"Why are they looking for you in the palace?" Uncle Pierce said. "Do you live in the palace? Are you part of the royal family?"

"No, not yet," the boy said, "and I hope I never will be, not if I can help it."

"Can we go somewhere else and talk?" I asked, uncomfortable in this hiding place.

"You need to tell us everything," Uncle Pierce said firmly.

"I don't have to tell you anything!" the boy shouted defiantly. He pushed against a wall, letting in light from the outside, stepped through a crack, and he was gone. The opening disappeared, as if it were not even there.

"What are we going to do now?" I asked, standing with my uncle in semi-darkness, in a strange place where the air smelled stale and stinky, under the threat of 'really getting in trouble' if we were to go out of here, trying not to panic.

"It looks to me like we have two choices," Uncle Pierce said with a sigh. "We can either stay here, or we can go out, the same way that boy went, and find some answers."

"We can't stay here," I said, shaking my head.

"So, let's go," Uncle Pierce, placing his hand lightly on my shoulder to get me going in the right direction.

I stepped over to the wall where the boy had created an opening and I pushed. I pushed harder until I was using all my strength, but the wall was not about to budge. Uncle Pierce stepped over beside me and we both began pushing as hard as we could. I turned around so I had my back against the wall, using the strength in my legs to push, but nothing was happening.

"How did he open it?" I asked, grunting, still pushing. I was trying to not think about being trapped inside this place, wondering if we could climb up the slide and go back into that closet in the prince's room.

"There must be a button or trigger around here somewhere," Uncle Pierce said. We stopped pushing and started hunting for it, feeling around on the wall and floor near where the boy had been standing when we last saw him, but we couldn't find a thing.

"How are we going to get out of here?" I asked, aware that my voice was much higher than normal, although I was trying my best to not sound like I was scared.

"Don't worry, Layla," Uncle Pierce said reassuringly, and I felt his hand patting on my shoulder. "We will be out of here before you know it. Then we will go and find your father."

Ah, those were sweet words to my ear, words that I wanted to believe and hoped with all my heart. As I thought of my dad, another thought popped into my head.

"Maybe this would be a good time for us to say a

prayer," I suggested.

"It surely couldn't hurt," Uncle Pierce said. "Why don't you pray?"

I thought about what my dad would say to God in a moment like this. Then I looked into my heart, because I felt that was where my prayer should come from, not from words my dad would use were he in this situation.

"My dear heavenly Father," I began, already feeling a blanket of peace come over my entire self, "we are in Your hands, and You know exactly where we are. I know You are able to take care of us, and You can get us out of this place. Thank You for what You have already done, bringing me to my dad and my uncle, and for bringing us safely across the world to this area. I don't even know where we are, but You know. Now, Father, if it is Your will, I ask that You show us the way out of here. If that is not Your will, for us to get out of this dark place, I pray that You give us peace while we are here. I love You, Lord, and I thank You. In the name of Jesus I pray. Amen."

"Thank you, Layla, that was a very nice prayer," Uncle Pierce said quietly. "Where did you learn to pray like that?"

I slid to the ground, so I was sitting on the floor, and I had never felt such a sense of relief. "I just told God what is in my heart," I said.

Uncle Pierce sat beside me, shifting and moving as he settled to the floor. "We are not cold, we are not injured. We have every reason to be thankful."

"Yes, we do," I agreed.

"Are you hungry?" he asked, moving things around a bit.

"Maybe a little," I said, suddenly aware that I was actually very hungry.

"I have some snack bites in my pack," he said, unzipping his backpack and pulling something out of it. He placed several small items into my hand.

"Thank you," I said, as I unwrapped one of the little packets. Remembering the weird fish we had had back at Mountain Veil, I was a little apprehensive. I smelled it, listening to Uncle Pierce munching away happily, and I popped one of them into my mouth. I was pleasantly surprised that it tasted very good, a chewy combination of nuts and grains. I kept chewing and chewing, and that one little bite was really filling me up. I put another one in my mouth, and as I was chewing on that one, a wave of sleepiness began to come over me.

"Are you tired?" Uncle Pierce asked, putting his arm around me, letting me lean against him.

Before I could even answer, I swallowed the remainder of the snack bites I had in my mouth and fell into a deep sleep.

CHAPTER 7

When I awakened, at first I had no idea where I was, nor how long I had been asleep. My head felt foggy and heavy, and although my first desire was to go to back to sleep, a sense of urgency was compelling me to pull myself fully awake.

"Uncle Pierce?" I said, my voice raspy and faint. My mouth felt like it was full of fabric, I was so thirsty. I felt around for my backpack and took out my container of water. The first drops were absorbed so quickly, I almost didn't need to even swallow. Before I drank all my water, though, I stopped, wondering how soon we would be able to find a bathroom. As my eyes adjusted to the darkness, I saw that Uncle Pierce seemed to be sound asleep beside me.

I needed to get out of this place, so I scooted over to the end of the slide where we had escaped from the prince's closet and began to crawl up it. It was very slippery, so I was only able to move very slowly, using my shoes to keep me from sliding backwards as I inched up, bit by bit.

"Layla!" Uncle Pierce suddenly shouted frantically, and I could hear him moving about.

"I am right here, Uncle Pierce," I said. "I am trying to climb up the slide. We have to get out of here."

"Have you gotten far?" he asked, coming closer to me.

"Not yet, but I am making progress," I said, moving a bit more, then sliding back involuntarily. "Well, it is not easy," I admitted.

"I don't think that is the best way to go," he said.

"But we have to get out of here!" I repeated, strengthening my efforts to move up the slide.

"I agree with you there," he said, "but now that we have gotten a bit of rest, let us continue to look for that trigger to open up the wall."

In the dim light, I could see him moving near the wall. I let myself glide back down to the bottom of the slide and joined my uncle in the search. My hands were feeling everywhere in the area where I recalled the boy had been, trying to find the slightest indentation, button, slot, or anything that could be pushed, pulled or poked. As I stepped to my left, I nearly tripped over something on the floor. I stumbled, stepping right on it, whatever it was, and, like magic, the wall began to open.

"There it is!" Uncle Pierce shouted, stepping through the crack.

I quickly followed him out of the darkness and the wall slid closed again.

"Whew!" I said. "That was close!" My backpack had barely made it through the crevice before the wall had closed and the opening disappeared.

My eyes were hurting as they adjusted to the extreme brightness. We were standing in a small crevice at the bottom of the canyon, way down at one end. To our right, the canyon ended in a natural wall, a curved rock wall that joined to the other side of the canyon. The layers of the wall were absolutely beautiful, with a variety of clay colors: reds, peaches, dark and light tans and browns, and with textures that could only have been created by God. Uncle Pierce hesitantly stepped out of the crevice, into the area that had looked, from above, like a movie set of a lane in one of the Before Time towns. People dressed in red were all over the place, moving back and forth, up and down the lane, and I could feel a sense of excitement as they chattered, laughed and kind of danced as they moved. No one took any notice of us, two strangers who were not dressed in the required red of the day, as we slowly walked down the lane. The ground where we were walking looked to be made of a natural rock, flattened down by wear, or perhaps smoothed by water thousands of years ago.

"Are we in the Grand Canyon?" I asked Uncle Pierce, remembering the stories Big Hawk had told, and the research we had done on that area of the land.

"I don't think so," Uncle Pierce said. "I think it was much bigger than this, longer, and much more grand."

"I think this is pretty grand," I said, noting the man-made additions of gold and carvings to the natural beauty of the rock in the canyon walls.

"The Grand Canyon was somewhat destroyed during the giant disaster," Uncle Pierce said, "so, actually, this could be a small portion of it. But, really, I think we are much farther south, perhaps in the area where the country of Mexico once was."

"We called it The Great Devastation," I said, "when the world was destroyed by both man and nature. Well, it wasn't completely destroyed, you know that, but it was changed forever."

"Yes, indeed," Uncle Pierce said, nodding and looking around us. "We need to find someone who is in charge, so we can find your father and your friends."

"It kind of looks like lots of people are going that way," I said, pointing to the opposite end of the canyon, where the walls of the canyon were very close together. Although people were going in all directions, many of them seemed to be lining up and going through this narrow crack in the landscape, like grains of sand going through the narrow part of an hourglass.

"Excuse me," Uncle Pierce said to a passing woman.

She completely ignored him, as if he had not even spoken, as she went about her business, crossing through the crowds of people.

"Are we invisible or something?" I asked with a little laugh.

"Maybe she couldn't hear me," Uncle Pierce suggested.

"So, should we shout it out, really loudly, or should we just follow everyone who is going in that direction?" I asked, curious as to what was happening through there.

"Wow, take a look at the palace," Uncle Pierce said, stopping in his tracks and looking up and over our heads.

Now that we were a distance away from the closer side of the canyon, we were able to get a look at the outside of the place the boy had called a palace, where we had just been. The entire side of the canyon was decorated with an enormous mosaic of colorful stones and gold and silver. The palace was carved into the rock, several stories high, with tall windows, doors, balconies on three levels, so it looked like a huge high-rise building embedded into the canyon wall.

I stepped backwards to get a better look, and I crashed into a young girl who must have been about my age. We both fell to the ground.

"I'm sorry," I said. "Are you okay?"

She looked at me and I saw anger on her face turn to fright, then she seemed to relax as she examined me. I was a little relieved to know that we were not invisible to these people.

She nodded, still looking at me, as Uncle Pierce helped her to her feet.

"Where is everyone going?" I asked, noting that this great lane was rapidly becoming deserted as people were being funneled out of here.

"To the wedding!" she said, eyeing my clothing. "Why are you not dressed for it?"

"We just got here," I said, hoping to start a conversation that would give us some answers.

"Who is getting married?" Uncle Pierce asked.

"Why, the princes, of course," she said. "Have you two been locked away? Everyone knows about the wedding of the princes."

"The princes are getting married?" I asked.

"Yes, today is the day we have all been waiting for!" she exclaimed.

"To each other?" I said, confused.

"Ha ha ha ha ha ha!" she laughed. "You really have been locked away if you think that!"

"You are saying, then, it is to be a double wedding?" Uncle Pierce asked.

A memory choked my throat: my parents and Uncle Pierce and Aunt Moon had had a double wedding. I remembered seeing the photos of the two beautiful brides, dressed in their beautiful white gowns, and the two young men with big smiles on their faces, so handsome in their black and white suits; the twin bouquets, the twin wedding cakes; the happiness that permeated from the photos to my memory of my childhood, before The Great Devastation.

"Yes, you can call it that," she said, nodding. "We call it the Wedding of the Princes. I am surprised you don't know that." She gave me a look that said she was somehow superior because she knew that fact and we didn't.

"Who are they marrying?" I asked.

"The two sisters!" she said. "Come on, we don't want to be late!"

She made a beeline toward the narrow opening, and we stayed right on her heels. Hundreds of others were also heading that way.

I had a really bad feeling about the whole thing, but we were swept up in the excitement. The thought occurred to me that Uncle Pierce would not get the opportunity to speak to the princes on their wedding day, but maybe, with everyone coming together, we would be able to find my dad, Kenrick, Nadir and Lena.

"Hey!" a male voice shouted, startling me. "You two are not dressed for the wedding!"

Uncle Pierce and I stopped and turned to see a man dressed in a red uniform, staring angrily right at us. My heart began to pound, something it had been doing a lot lately, since we had started on this adventure. All we needed was to be arrested and locked up, like the young girl had mentioned.

"This is all we have," Uncle Pierce said, holding up his hands to show that we were not holding our wedding outfits in our hands.

"So, go and get your appropriate clothing!" the man

said. He must have noticed the confusion on our faces as he pointed to one of the stores that was over behind us now. "You better hurry, if you want to make it before the ceremony starts!"

Uncle Pierce and I exchanged glances as we stepped sideways, out of the crowd that was flowing toward the narrow opening.

"Yeah, sure," Uncle Pierce said. "Thanks for the reminder."

We hurried over to the door of the place where the man had just directed us to come and stepped inside what seemed to be an old fashioned shop full of clothing. However, this one was different. I could remember going to the Mall Quadrant with my mom and Aunt Moon, and each store had clothing for men or women or children. This place was filled with clothing, beautifully displayed, for all ages of people, but the outfits were sorted by color. Near the front window all the clothing was white, behind the white clothing were the yellow clothes, then was a section of orange clothing. Next was the red section, so we hurried over to find something that would fit us. I had no idea of what style to choose: everything here looked to be very fancy.

"Maybe someone can help us," I said, looking around the store for anyone who worked there.

"I don't see anyone in here," Uncle Pierce said. He was much taller than I, so he could see over the clothing racks. "We will have to help ourselves."

"How are we going to pay for it?" I asked.

"Let's just borrow something red for the wedding, and when it is over, we can bring the red things back and change back to our clothes. We are not going to keep these outfits."

That made sense to me, especially since we were in a hurry, but first I had to find a bathroom. I stepped behind a curtain and found a crude rest room – a hole in the floor. From the odor, I knew instantly that this was their type of bathroom. I quickly relieved myself and got out of there. As I was approaching the cluster of red clothing, I saw a really nice red outfit hanging near the wall that looked like it might be my size.

"Can we just change into these, and take them?" I asked, still unsure about this whole process.

"Looks like we are going to have to, in order to go to the wedding," Uncle Pierce said, going through some of the red items on one of the men's racks.

"Do we have to go to the wedding?" I asked, feeling very uncomfortable.

"I think we should," he said. "I don't know why, but I really feel like we need to be there. I just have this strange feeling, way down inside of me."

I knew he was right, I felt something, too, but I was reluctant to just put on these clothes and walk out without earning them.

"Come on, Layla, hurry," he said, already pulling a long red jacket over his other clothes.

I grabbed the red outfit from its hanger and stepped behind a large divider so I could change my clothes with privacy. I pulled off my other clothes and stuffed them into my backpack. I was amazed how well the red outfit fit me. It seemed to just glide right onto me and the fabric felt so smooth, like none other I had ever felt. As I caught a glimpse of myself in a mirror, I was surprised at how I looked – not like myself, but like a nicely dressed young lady. I tried to smooth my curly hair and then came out from behind the divider.

Uncle Pierce looked very debonair in all red! We both stopped and stared at each other for a moment before he called out to whomever may be listening, "We will bring them back!" We rushed out of the clothing shop and blended into the crowd that was on their way to the wedding.

As we were forced into single file due to the narrow width of the corridor, I happened to look up. On ledges, standing way above us, were lookout guards. Although they didn't seem to be paying any attention to the flow of humans leaking out of the canyon, I had a feeling that they usually were stationed there to prevent unwanted visitors from entering. That thought really gave me the creeps, as I wondered who they needed to keep out of here.

The crowd flowed toward a huge plain area, where an enormous throng of people was assembled, a giant quilt of red, spread across the desert. I was curious to see the brides and grooms, but nobody stood out of the crowd. We were on the outside of the multitude, in the back row. Everyone was facing toward a large rock that made a plateau, so I assumed the wedding party or parties would gather up there.

The sun was shining high in the turquoise blue sky, without a cloud in sight. We were standing on the most magnificent plain of nature, with orange clay rocky hills surrounding us in the distance, and very little plant life anywhere. Although the air was warm, I didn't feel hot in this red outfit. It must have been made out of some kind of fabric that prevented people from sweating.

Out of the corner of my eye, I saw the boy that we

had met earlier passing by us.

"Hey!" I said to him, waving at him.

He glanced in my direction but he acted as if he didn't even know me, as he continued walking around the crowd. I squeezed between the mass of people, pressing through here and there so I could catch up with him, hoping Uncle Pierce would follow me. When I finally caught up to the boy, I touched his arm.

"Hi," I said, suddenly not knowing what to say.

He looked me up and down before answering, "Hi."

"It's me!" I said, in case he hadn't noticed. I was relieved that Uncle Pierce was right beside me, and I motioned back and forth between him and me. "We changed into red clothes."

"You and everyone else," he said. "If you will excuse me, I am needed in the ceremony."

"You are in the ceremony?" I asked. "Why didn't you tell us that before?"

"Because I have never seen you before in my entire life," he said, stepping away from us, to continue on his journey to the back of the gigantic crowd.

"Wait!" I said, without trying to yell.

He turned his face to me again, while still walking away from us.

"We met you earlier today," Uncle Pierce said, "up on top of this canyon rim," then he lowered his voice, "and we sneaked through the palace."

The boy stopped and looked around at the crowd, possibly to see if anyone else was paying any attention to us. He quickly stepped over to us, getting right in our faces.

"That was not me! I have been busy all day, doing everything for my mom and the prince, while my lazy brother has been running around, getting in trouble, as usual!" He had a look of disgust on his face, a look so out of place on a child of his age.

"Is he going to be in the wedding, too?" I asked. I was getting excited, because I had never before attended a wedding, and I had no idea of what was going to happen. What a bonus to actually know someone who was going to be in the wedding!

"If they can find him!" he said angrily. "He is always running off and getting in trouble! I have to get going, now, or else I am going to be in trouble also."

He rushed away from us and I started to follow him. Uncle Pierce's hand on my shoulder stopped me. I looked up at him.

"Let him go," he said. "Let us prepare to watch this wedding, maybe from up there, where we can get a better view."

I looked to where the plain was a bit higher, off to our left, and some people were already going up there.

"Do you think he really has a brother?" I asked Uncle Pierce, while we were climbing up the incline. "Or did he just say that so he won't get in trouble for being where he wasn't supposed to be?"

"Does it really matter?" Uncle Pierce asked, shrugging his shoulders. "Come on, we should be able to see from over there."

We found a spot, along with hundreds of other people, where we could stand, that was overlooking the area where the ceremony was to take place. The entire crowd was facing a clearing, where a giant red carpet had been spread on the ground. An enormous brass disk was hanging from a frame at the back of the area. An item that looked like a curved doorway had been placed in the middle of the red carpet, and it was covered with red and white flowers. Two people were fussing about on the carpet, flattening it and sweeping it and picking up tiny unseen objects, presumably to make it as clean and smooth as possible. The audience stood around talking, a humming buzz of conversation, and everyone was acting really happy. I tried to estimate how many people were here, in this largest group of humans I had ever seen. The front row had about eighty people, and there were at least fifty rows: so, on that side alone, stood more than four thousand people. Add that to the several hundred who were up near us, and I concluded that the boy had been correct when he told us thousands of people lived here.

A man came out of the crowd with a large stick in his hand, a stick that had a huge ball on one end of it. He walked over to the big brass disk, lifted the stick over his head, and swung it down to hit the disk one time, making a loud musical sound that echoed back and forth. The crowd instantly hushed as the group split in two, parting down the center, revealing a long red carpet that had been hidden by people standing on it.

Everyone turned to face the back of the crowd, moving around to get a good view in that direction. With great anticipation, I strained to see where they were looking, back toward the crevice where we had been funneled, where the two sides of the canyon nearly came together. The air was filled with the sweet sound of music as musicians began to file out of the canyon area, playing their instruments. Although didn't have any live musicians back at the Complex, I had seen enough movies to recognize the flute, which came first, with a lady playing a solo that touched my very heart. She was followed by a man playing the violin that suddenly made me start to cry, the sound was so beautiful. They moved so gracefully across the desert floor, a slow and deliberate dance, up to the red carpet between the crowd, then over to the other side of the small plateau, where they rose up to the top and took their places on the red carpet. The volume of the music became more quiet as three guitar players, one woman and two men, emerged and joyfully strummed and danced their way, following the same route as the first musicians. As they joined the flute player and violinist, the music became very loud and jubilant.

Suddenly the music stopped and I was looking at those five musicians who seemed to be having the time of their lives, standing on that red carpet while holding their instruments. I was startled and I jumped when the explosion of drums bounced out of the crevice, and I turned to see two drummers appear. Before they got to the red carpet, two men playing trumpets came out, their trumpets proclaiming the beginning of a true celebration, and they followed the drummers up to where the other musicians were waiting. With all nine of them together, they began to play a lovely song, each taking turns with solos, then blending into such a beautiful song, growing very loud as they playfully enjoyed themselves. The entire crowd down below us got involved as everyone started clapping their hands to the beat. The effect was tremendous as the vibrations echoed around off the hills that surrounded us. The music was coming at us from all directions, beating, strumming, jamming, and it felt like it was moving my heart, coming from inside of me as well as outside of me. I was being swept away by the beautiful melody and harmony, as it grew louder and louder to a deafening crescendo – then abruptly stopped. The clapping stopped and the entire valley was filled with complete silence.

CHAPTER 8

Slowly, so quietly at first, the gentle sound of the strumming of strings floated out from the crevice, a sincere and heart-wrenching tune playing for several minutes before the appearance of a giant harp on a platform on wheels, with a lady leaning into the harp, plucking the strings passionately, as one man pulled and another pushed the platform unhurriedly across to the red carpet and up to the plateau, taking at least ten minutes to get from one end to the other. The rest of the musicians began to play softly to compliment the song of the harp.

When the music eventually stopped, the drums began to beat rapidly and the entire crowd seemed to inhale at the same time. I turned my attention back to the crevice, and I saw a little boy – not the same one (or two) we had seen earlier, but another boy about the same age and dressed all in red – marching, deliberately, across to the red carpet, all the way up the plateau, to stand under the flower-decorated doorway. A very gentle song was coming from the violin while we all stood in anticipation, watching and waiting for who would come next. A bit of laughter erupted in the crowd, but no one was coming.

Minutes passed. As we waited, something about the boy – or boys? – who had spoken to us was really bothering me. They looked and sounded exactly the same, but the way they acted was so different. They had both been dressed in fancy red outfits, but as I thought about it, the boy we had just seen, the second one, seemed to be a little better kept. His hair was neater and his clothes were not as wrinkled. This could have been because he had gone somewhere and straightened up for the wedding… yet the look in his eye told me that he had been telling us the truth, that he did have a twin brother.

Several minutes later, my conclusion was confirmed. Both boys, identical twins, burst out of the crevice, each trying to be first, pushing and shoving at each other until they finally straightened up, both looking straight ahead instead of at each other, and marched side-by-side across to the red carpet, through the crowd, to their places beside the other little boy. At that point, all three of them started giggling, laughing uncontrollably, bending over and holding their sides.

The drummers did a rapid beating of their drums, and the boys were instantly the picture of obedience as they looked toward the gap between the canyon walls. A woman dressed in royal attire – a purple flowing gown, trimmed in gold, with an enormous golden crown on her head, obviously the Queen – was escorted by a tall man, slowly, ceremoniously, as they made their way to their position under the flowered archway. The tall man had dark hair and was dressed in fancy clothing, all in black, with a shiny black vest over his black long sleeved shirt. As they strolled through the crowd, the Queen graciously nodded to the left and right at the people, and from where we were, I could see her smiling as she acknowledged them. She had a beautiful smile and a wide, round face with high cheekbones. She took her place, proud and confident, beside the boys, right in the middle of them, with the tall man standing beside her.

I turned to look at Uncle Pierce, only to see that he was scanning the crowd, searching for someone.

"Are you looking for my dad?" I whispered.

"What?" he asked, distracted and still looking. "No,

no; oh, yes, yes."

The sound of trumpets blasting turned my attention back to the wedding party as one of the princes stepped out of the crevice. I had no doubt that he was a prince, because he also was wearing a golden crown, one smaller than the Queen's, and his jacket was also purple with fancy gold trim. He was very tall and handsome, with striking features carved into his face. He was a little older than I had been expecting, especially after seeing how young the Queen looked.

As he walked down the red carpet, marching to the trumpet's beat, a young lady suddenly screamed loudly and lunged toward him.

"Prince Arumbo!" she shouted. Several men in the crowd quickly subdued her as she screamed, "No, no, he is mine! He is going to marry ME!" She was carried off to one side of the crowd, far away from the plateau, by three large men, as she kept yelling, "He is MY prince, let me go!" I had the feeling certain guards had been placed in the crowd in case of an incident such as this.

The prince continued his journey unaffected, although he did not greet the crowd as the Queen had, and he soon joined her, standing right under the archway. His eyes were fixed on the crevice, and another prince came walking gallantly out, dressed exactly the same as the first prince, and also extremely handsome. I almost expected a repeat of the screaming by another young lady, but this prince was allowed to walk the entire way without incident.

With most of the wedding party already in place, the musicians began to play again. I was really getting anxious to see the brides, to get on with the ceremony, but all I could do was wait and listen to the music – which seemed to be going on and on forever. Some people in the audience began to dance, so from where we stood, it gave the appearance of a giant pot of red boiling water, bubbling here and there. I kept looking back and forth from the wedding party, who were all standing calmly and smiling, to the crevice where nothing was happening, and still the music kept playing.

I wondered why Uncle Pierce was acting so strangely, and when the ceremony was going to continue. The top of my head was getting hot as the sun was beating down on us, and I was getting tired of standing. I was just looking to see if I could sit or maybe even squat on the ground when a hush fell over the crowd. The lady playing the harp began to pluck the strings, making the most heavenly music I had ever heard as all heads turned toward the crevice.

The first bride appeared, all dressed in a very pale lavender color, with a veil covering her whole head. She moved slowly and carefully across the sand, over the red carpet, and up to the plateau. She took her place beside one of the princes. I was surprised at how the lavender was complimented by all that red, but it did look very nice.

The second bride was already halfway through the crowd when I saw her. I wasn't sure if I spent too much time examining the first bride, or if the second bride didn't wait until her proper time, but there she was, also in pale lavender and with a veil over her head, already walking up to meet her prince. I was smiling to myself, thinking of two sisters marrying two brothers who were princes, and how this was almost like a fairy tale from the olden days.

"We will now have a musical selection to begin the

wedding ceremony," the tall man who was standing beside the Queen announced. I was very surprised at how well his voice carried, because he didn't seem to be shouting, but it looked as though everyone could hear him. I decided it must have been due to the acoustics of the area, and the shape of the valley.

The musicians began to play another song, and people in the crowd again began to dance. I noticed that the members of the wedding party were standing still as a stick, though, and the ones who were up with us were not moving about much either. The song went on for quite some time, and I was really getting tired of standing. I bent over at the waist, just for some relief, and reached to touch the rocky surface beneath our feet. Next, I squatted for a moment, stretching the muscles of my back. When I stood up again, I twisted from side to side, back and forth, longing to be able to sit down, when finally, the music subsided and stopped.

With all attention turned to the wedding party, the tall man stepped out in front of the others.

"We are glad to have you all here today," he said, addressing the crowd. "We are gathered here today to join these two couples in marriage, two princes to two sisters, right here, today, in the sight of all of our community." He stepped to the side and held out his hand to showcase the two couples. "We first would like to hear the declaration from our Queen."

The crowd applauded respectfully as the Queen took a step forward.

"I want to personally thank each and every one of you for coming here to be with us today," she said graciously, sounding somewhat like a recording.

"We are here today to celebrate the joining in

marriage of my two sons, Prince Arumbo and Prince Botolo, to these two lovely young ladies." She paused as she nodded to each prince and each lovely young lady. "As you are aware, these two sisters were chosen specifically to become the next princesses of our community because of their honesty, their loyalty, their respect for the positions and the love of my sons toward them."

I briefly wondered if the two lovely young ladies had love toward these two princes, but didn't have much time to consider it before a shout from the crowd interrupted my train of thought.

"And because they have sons!" The crowd ignored her, the same lady who had been shouting at the prince, the only person who seemed to be in objection to this double wedding.

A different thought came into my mind, and that was that there were no other children here besides the three boys. I quickly looked all around, but those were the only young children in the entire crowd, and I could see just about everyone from the raised plateau where I stood. There were quite a few teenagers, but no little kids, and no babies.

"We shall be honored to have these two lovely young ladies join our family and join us in the palace as part of the royal family. We have invited all of you to witness this historic celebration, to be a part of the joy and the fellowship, as we make history on this day, a day that will long be remembered in our memories and in the official records of our community. We all know that it has not been an easy journey for us to get where we are today, but we have been taking the journey together, step by step, one step at a time, from where we were then to where we are now, and it has not been easy, but we have been able to do it only because we have been working together.

"When we think back to the beginning of this journey, we had struggles and strife, hardships and sufferings. We could not have come this far, to the point where we are today, if we had not come together, and planned together, and worked together, to make this community what it is today. We have laughed and cried together. We have worked side by side, and it has not been easy. We have been able to do together what none of us could ever have been able to do alone. We have placed one stone upon another, taken one step at a time, using our combined wisdom and strength. Without each other, we could not even imagine that we could possibly be right here, where we are, right here today."

I was beginning to wonder exactly where we were, not only here today, but right here, within the Queen's long-winded speech.

"My dear friends," she continued, "I know you and you know me. We are in this together, both yesterday and today and tomorrow, and we can only keep going forward and achieving greater and greater heights if we continue to work together. Oh, and our lives are not only all about working together. We have made our lives wonderful by living together, playing together, singing together, dancing together, and celebrating together!"

At this, the crowd cheered, and I had a strange feeling that this was one of those standard speeches given by the Queen that they had all heard before, so they knew exactly when to be quiet and when to react.

"So, as I was saying, we are gathered here together on this wonderful, beautiful, historic day to celebrate!"

Again, the crowd cheered, yelling, shouting,

whistling and clapping.

"We are not here to dwell on the bad times we had in the past," the Queen said. "We are here to draw strength from ourselves and each other, to propel our community into the future, starting with today, when we shall all have a day of celebration, and in the future we can look back at this day and say that this day, this very day, truly was a wonderful day, a day like none other."

Was any day like another? I wondered, hoping she would get to the point of her speech and then finish it.

"We have all set aside our daily routines in order to be here, right here, at this specific place, at this specific time, so we can witness the greatest of all occasions: the occasion of the double marriage of my sons, Prince Arumbo and Prince Botolo, to these two lovely ladies who are standing up here, beside my sons. This day will go down in history, will be written by our historians, and this day will be remembered by us. We will tell of this day often, so the memory will not be lost, not among us, not today, not in our lifetimes, not ever. We will remember this celebration and we will celebrate the memory of this celebration, and that celebration will become a celebration of the memory of each celebration."

I was trying to follow what the Queen was saying, but I wasn't sure she even knew where she was going with this line of non-logic. I just wanted her to get finished and get on with the celebration – unless they were only planning to celebrate the memory of a celebration of a memory of a celebration.

"I would like to individually thank each and every one of you," the Queen said, and I hoped she did not mean that literally. "I look out at your faces, the faces of people I have been seeing every day, faces of hard workers and faces of generous friends. I would have no greater pleasure than if I could call out each of your names, individually, because each of you is an individual, and, as a collection of individuals, you make up this group, this community."

She stopped speaking for a few minutes to nod her head about a hundred times, looking directly at individuals as she nodded.

"I see the love and kindness in your eyes, and feel your support with every breath that you take. You cannot possibly know how much you all mean to me, because you all do mean so much to me. Here you are, standing out here on this historic day, showing me your love and support, standing with me and my sons, and this does mean so much to me, and, although we have not discussed it, I know it means so much to my sons as well. I can tell by the look on their faces that they also feel your love and support, and so this means so much to each of us, to each one of us, individually, and to each of us as a group, as a family, together, as one."

She paused and glanced back at her sons, presumably to confirm that they did indeed feel the love and support of this entire crowd on this historic day.

"Now, as you know, moving ahead and going further, we hope that we all will know and stand on what will be best for us as a community. We can learn from our mistakes of the past, but let us learn by not dwelling on and repeating those mistakes, but by learning what makes us stronger and more efficient and sticks us together like glue, as we go forward, onward and upward, as a community that is committed to going forward together, supporting each other, and working together, so we can again have reasons to celebrate!"

The word 'celebrate' must have been the applause trigger, because there they went again, exploding in applause, even though in my opinion, the Queen had yet to make her point. People were jumping up and down, really ready to celebrate. How were they going to react when the ceremony was actually finished and the real celebration was to begin?

"And as we all know, or you may not know, or you may or may not know, depending on whether you know or not, and if you don't know, you should know, that is if you want to know, then you really should make it a point to know that we as a community are unlike any other community, either past, present, or future, and especially present, but also in the past, and we, as a community, need to hold each other up, and be together, as a community, because the community is made up of individuals, but individual individuals are not a community unless they are a community. This is why we need to work together as a community, as individuals coming together as a community, because we are not alone, we are a community. We are not just a group of individuals out in space, individual islands, so to speak, all to ourselves, but we are individuals who are in a community, each giving our individual self to this community, and that's what makes us a community.

"That is what makes us the greatest community, and the only community of its kind, with none other like it, past, present, or future, so if you did not know, now you know and if you did not want to know you still know, whether you wanted to know or if you did not want to know. So, this is what makes us so great. We are a great community, and today, we have a real reason to celebrate!"

There they went with the applause again, although

I was still trying to figure out what was the point of the speech.

"In conclusion, as you know and may not already have known and now as you have come to know, we are a great community and this is a great day for our great community, and I am so happy that each and every one of you is here to be a part of this community on this great day, so we can, individually, come together as a community, to take part in this great day, this great event, on this memorable day that we shall never forget, as the great day when we all came together to celebrate, together, as individuals who live in a community together and who love to live and celebrate together!"

Now came the loudest cheering and applause, as if she had said something really great; however, since I had never lived under the rule of a queen, maybe I did not really understand their sentiments. The Queen nodded her head toward the group on her left, then toward the group on her right, and finally, toward us, the ones up on the other plateau. The cheering went on for several minutes until finally the tall man stepped forward and raised his palms to the crowd. Instantly the entire place was silent.

"As you know, our custom during a wedding is to pass the ceremonial cup," he said. He pulled a golden cup out from under his vest and held it up for the crowd to see – another applause trigger – and the crowd went wild. He then held it up to his lips, as if he were taking a drink, and passed it to the Queen, who did the same. She gave it to Prince Arumbo, who put it to his lips and passed it to Prince Botolo, who repeated the ritual. He passed the cup to one of the musicians, who handed it to the next musician, and so on, until everyone who was on the plateau had held it, including the three boys, but excluding the two brides, who still had their faces covered by their veils.

One of the boys handed the cup to a person in the front row of the audience, and I was dismayed to see that this cup was to be passed around to each and every person standing in this assembly. My legs were killing me as I shifted from one foot to the other, unaccustomed to standing for such a length of time. When I let out a sigh, I tried to not let it be too loud, but this ceremonial ritual was really putting a strain on me. Now I could understand why the Queen had said that this would be a day to be remembered. This wedding ceremony had already lasted more than an hour, and nothing had really happened yet. What would be next, each person folding a piece of paper until it could be stacked up to the moon?

When the cup finally reached me, seemingly days later, I had no desire to touch it to my lips, so I just held it up near my lips and then gave it to Uncle Pierce, who was next in line beside me. He did the same thing as I had done and quickly passed the cup to the next person. The look on his face told me that he was as confused as I was, but what could we do besides go along with what everyone else was doing?

When the ritual of the ceremonial cup was finished and the final person had given the cup back to the man in black, he stood in front of the crowd and smiled. I held my breath, hoping that this was not going to be his turn for another meaningless speech, but he just stayed there for a few moments, smiling out at the crowd. Just about everyone in the audience was smiling back at him, making me think they were all experiencing heat stroke or something, but he finally raised his arms, palms up to the sky for a few seconds, then he dropped his hands and turned to face the wedding party. He stepped between them and turned around so he was facing the crowd with the wedding party just in front of him, with the men on his left, the little boys standing off beyond them and the two brides on his right. The Queen was now sitting in the only chair in sight, and I had no idea who had brought it up to the plateau for her.

"Friends of all kinds," the man began, "we are here to witness the joining of this man and this woman, and this man and this woman --"

As he said it, a gentle laughter arose from the crowd as the two brides exchanged places, having been lined up with the incorrect grooms, but who could tell, since they still had their faces covered?

"As I was saying, we might as well just declare them to be married," the man said. "Do I hear any objection? We can begin the festivities now, as I declare, you are now married!"

"Wait a minute!" a man's voice called out, a very familiar voice. "What about joining in holy matrimony? What about the blessings of God?"

I stood on tiptoe to see the source of the voice, which I recognized to be my dad's voice! I could not locate him in the sea of red, but now, I was so relieved! I knew he was here!

CHAPTER 9

"We don't have any type of religious person in our community," the tall man on the plateau said, using a voice that indicated that everyone knew that. "Our community has renounced all types of religion, since it is old fashioned and out of date. We have no religion!"

"We do now!" my dad called, and I saw him push through the crowd, to make his way to the platform.

I was beaming, knowing that my dad was doing the right thing, making this wedding what it should be: a marriage in the sight of God, according to God's ordinances. I wanted to get closer to him, but because of the enormous mob between him and me, I decided to just stay back and watch from this excellent viewpoint that I had.

As my dad approached the wedding party and the sun was now directly over our heads, I began to feel a little dizzy – and I wasn't the only one. One of the brides suddenly collapsed, falling right into her sister's arms. They both melted slowly to the ground. A collective gasp came from the audience as the princes fell to their knees, hovering over their brides, and the crowd pressed forward, threatening to surround the ones on the plateau.

"Give them some air!" the tall man shouted.

I could not see a thing on the ceremonial plateau, since so many people were moving closer and closer to the wedding party. I looked up at Uncle Pierce, but he was no longer beside me. I frantically began to search for him before deciding I had to get to my dad right away, no matter what else was happening.

"You need to get back!" the man shouted. "In the name of the Queen, give the royal wedding party some room!"

Before I knew what was happening, I saw that Uncle Pierce was up on the plateau, and two very large men were trying to restrain him. They were able to get him in a tight hold, and he began flailing his arms and legs in an attempt to free himself from their grip. My dad was also being pulled away from the royal wedding party by two hefty men. My dad, too, was protesting violently, as they pulled him in the other direction, away from the wedding party and away from me. I had to get over there, to be with my dad and my uncle, but the crowd was too thick, as they pressed together more and more tightly, and I could barely move.

"I declare that the double wedding of Prince Arumbo and Prince Botolo is over, they have their brides, and we shall now begin the great and memorable celebration!" the tall man shouted loudly, over the roaring of the crowd.

This time, the word 'celebration' did not trigger applause but a sudden silence.

"The prince cannot marry this bride!" my dad shouted, as he was being pulled further and further away from the wedding plateau.

"We refuse to attach any religious significance to this ceremony! This wedding is over and the princes are now married!" the tall man said forcefully. The crowd began to move in on my dad, growing louder and louder, and I was afraid they were going to crush him because he had a different belief than they had.

"She is already married!" my dad shouted at the top of his lungs.

CHAPTER 10

A loud hush fell over the entire crowd.

"And so is her sister!" Uncle Pierce shouted, trying frantically to break loose from the grip those two men had on him.

"What are you talking about?" Prince Arumbo asked, standing up to his full height. "Both of their late husbands are long dead. They died before their sons were born, before we even set up this community!"

My mind was going click-click-click as everything began to make sense to me. My dad and Uncle Pierce must have gotten a look under the veils, at the faces of the two brides. One of the brides – the one who fainted when she heard my dad's voice – was my mother, and the other bride was my Aunt Moon! That explained why the boy and I were arguing, when Uncle Pierce had said, like brother and sister – because we were! The boy's twin was my other brother, and the other boy was my cousin! I had two brothers! At the time of the Great Devastation, both my mother and my aunt had been pregnant. They must have escaped from the people who were in control at the Complex, or perhaps they had escaped before they even knew they were pregnant. In any case, my mom and my Aunt Moon had been living here, hiding from the ones at the Complex, who would have taken their sons away from them.

Right over there, almost within reach, was my mother! I had not seen her since they had stripped me from her and had taken me to the Complex, nine years ago! I had to get to her. The crowds were enormous, crushing, all pressing together and I could not get through to them to be near her.

"Mom!" I called out; but my one word was drowned out by the yelling and shouting of the masses. I looked to where my dad had been, but he was no longer there; he and Uncle Pierce both had been taken away. I was so alone in this giant crowd, I did not know what to do or where to go. All I could do was be pushed this way and pulled that way, as I was riding along on the wave of people who were also deciding where they were going.

I looked back up to the plateau where, just a few short minutes ago, the wedding party had been standing in front of the musicians. Now the plateau was empty! I could not see either of the brides nor the boys nor the Queen and her princes. I frantically searched the crowd, but they had vanished! The musicians had come down from the plateau and were standing off to one side, carefully guarding their instruments, protecting them from the moving multitude. Who was protecting my mother, and where had they taken her?

Kenrick had been right when he had told me he had found my mother. Kenrick had to be here, because last time I saw him, he was with my dad, and my dad was here! All I needed to do was to find Kenrick. I knew he would be able to help me locate my mom and my aunt and also my dad and uncle. I could always depend on Kenrick… if I could just find him.

What would be the best way to find a friend in this massive throng of thousands of people? I needed to get up onto the plateau, where I could speak and my voice would carry, and then Kenrick would be able to find me. We would be able to make our plan, and everything would work out perfectly, I just knew it. I was holding on tight to that hope, telling myself that I was confident my plan would work, as I squeezed and pushed and prodded myself toward the plateau. As I was getting very close to it, I felt a hand on my shoulder, holding me back, preventing me from taking another step. A sudden feeling of doom fell over me, and I tried to think of any kind of plan to get me out of this mess and over to where I needed to be.

CHAPTER 11

"Layla!" a male voice said, and I was immediately relieved.

I turned to see Nadir standing behind me, dressed in red, and I lost all control of my emotions as I fell against him and began to sob. He encircled me with his long and steady arms.

I tried to speak but instead it came out as blubber, about my mom, my dad, my twin brothers. Nadir just held my head against his chest and let me go on, not trying to make sense of it or even say anything. When I was finally able to breathe without shuddering, he stroked my hair and said, "It is going to be all right." Now the two of us were standing in the midst of a crowd gone wild, but I was no longer alone, and my hopes became real again.

I looked up at him. "We have to find my dad," I said, "and then we have to find my mom."

He gave me a funny look, then he looked to his side. Lena was standing right there, and I instantly felt uncomfortable being in such an extended hug with Nadir while Lena was watching. I stepped back a couple of inches, as far as I could go with the mob pressing in on us.

"We will find your father," Lena assured me. At that moment, I realized that they did not know that my mom was one of the brides, and Aunt Moon was the other one. How could they know? I had just figured it out, and I hadn't actually gotten a look at either of their faces.

"We need to talk," I said, looking for a way out of the crowd, where we could have a bit of privacy. I began examining the faces as they were passing by us. "Where is Kenrick, anyway?"

"He say he will come back," Lena said. "He must to go to work. He go to find you after he finish his work. He leave us here with your father to find your mother. He tell us to not worry about him."

Kenrick was the last person in the world I would ever need to spend any time worrying about. Although he was so young, he was so smart, and he had everything under control. Such an odd feeling came over me when I considered that Kenrick was still working at the Complex – and for the Complex. My life had expanded so far beyond those restrictive walls that I could not imagine ever returning to that kind of world. I really felt sorry for him.

Yet, at this moment, I had to focus on much more important things – finding my parents. I had been so close to both of them, and they had been physically taken away from me, right before my eyes! My dad and Uncle Pierce had been pulled in one direction, and my mom and Aunt Moon had been ushered in another direction.

"Let's go over there," I said, pointing back to the ledge where Uncle Pierce and I had been watching the wedding – or the prelude to what could have been a wedding – which was now just about bare. The three of us fought against the wave of people rolling in the opposite direction until we were able to get through them and climb up onto the rocky surface.

"I have to tell you something," I said, keeping my voice low, so only Nadir and Lena could hear me. They looked at me with anticipation.

"My mom and my Aunt Moon are both here, living

in this community," I began, already speaking rapidly. Their eyes just about popped out of their heads.

"You did see your mother here, in these people?" Lena interrupted.

"Where is she?" Nadir said. "Let us go to her now!"

"No, I didn't see her," I said, trying to figure out the best way to tell them, "I mean, I did see her, but I didn't see her face."

"How you do recognize a person and not see her face?" Nadir asked.

"You cannot be positive if you do not see the face," Lena added.

"You did see your aunt?" Nadir asked.

"Hold it, hold it!" I said. We were all blabbing - they were not letting me tell them. "The two brides, the ones in the wedding, one is my mom and the other one is my Aunt Moon."

Nadir and Lena looked at me, speechless.

"And there is more," I said quickly. "I have two brothers, the two twins that were standing up with the wedding party, and the other little boy is my cousin."

"You never saw your brothers before," Nadir stated.

"I did not know I had twin brothers until today! They were born after The Great Devastation! I did not know my mom was pregnant, I don't know if she even knew!" I exclaimed, being careful to keep my voice low. "I met one of my brothers earlier – we met him, Uncle Pierce and I did, and he is the one who brought us down into the canyon, back over there, where everyone is going through, and that is where we saw the palace and where we got our red clothing."

"So, your brother did tell you that your mother is here?" Nadir asked.

"No, when we were talking to him I did not yet realize he is my brother," I sighed. "I think he knew I am his sister, because when I told him my name, he started to act really funny. And I did not know he had a twin."

"What your brother name is called?" Lena asked.

"I don't know!" I said, frustrated. "We asked him but he would not tell us his name."

"I am not understanding," Nadir said, shaking his head. "You do not know the name of your brother and you did not see the face of your mother. How you do know for sure this is your brother, and these are your two twin brothers, and this is your mother in the wedding?"

"I knew it when my dad and my Uncle Pierce shouted out that the brides are already married! That is why the one bride fainted, when she heard my dad's voice."

"No, I think she stands too long in the sun and gets dizzy," Nadir said.

"Well, we have to find her, and we have to find my dad, and we have to get my family all together!" I insisted. At this moment, I did not have time to explain everything logically, we just had to get busy and find out where they had been taken.

"We must make plan," Nadir said, the first reasonable idea he had.

"Yes, yes, that is what I have been saying!" I said, nodding my head in agreement.

"First, we must find out where they have taken your

father," Nadir said. "Next, we take your father to your mother and your family is all together. After this, we find way to go back to Sammy and Salwa. From that place, we go to find what did happen to fathers of Lena and Salwa."

"Where we are going to live?" Lena asked, with a look of worry on her face. "Do we live in the mountain or in military compound under the ground with our fathers or we do bring them here to live?"

"Wait, wait!" I said. "Just a minute! We have to focus on what we are doing here, now! We have to find out where my dad is and go to him, before we can do anything else! He will know what to do after that. So, we have to make a plan on how we are going to find him."

"You can ask a person where he is?" Lena suggested.

"That's a good idea, but who can we ask?" I said, looking around at the dwindling crowd. Many of the people had already returned to the canyon area where the palace was; as a matter of fact, there was quite a long line of people waiting to go through the narrow crevice to get back inside there.

"We will ask the Queen," Nadir suggested.

"Yeah, as if she could ever answer a question," I said sarcastically, thinking of her nonsensical speech.

"What you are talking about?" Lena asked sincerely.

I smiled at her. "I don't think we will be able to approach the Queen. They probably have her locked up in the palace by now, away from this embarrassment of an incident. Well, she was right about one thing. This will be a day they will never forget."

"Where the children are?" Lena asked, as she looked

over at the people who were standing in line.

"What children?" I asked, confused.

"Lena is correct," Nadir said. "We saw only three boys, but no other children today."

"Maybe they are somewhere else?" I guessed.

"Why all children are to be somewhere else?" Lena asked.

"That is a very good question," I said. "After we find my dad and my mom, we will ask someone about that."

"Something very strange happens in this place," Nadir said, and, despite the heat of the overhead sun pounding down on us, I saw him shiver.

"You are right about that," I said, suddenly getting a very strange feeling. "Let's follow everyone into the canyon. They must have taken my dad and Uncle Pierce in there, because where else could they have gone?"

"They may go anywhere in this very great desert," Nadir said, a statement I did not want to hear, as we both gazed at the expanse to our left and right.

By the time we caught up to the rest of the crowd, we were the last three people in line. We were the only ones who were still outside the canyon, except for the musicians, who were taking care of their instruments.

I pulled up my courage and tapped the man in front of us on the shoulder.

"Yes?" he said, as he turned to me, smiling. "Would you care to go in front of me?"

"No, no thank you," I began, but before I could continue, he interrupted me.

"Then what can I do for you, my dear?" he said, with a creepy overtone to his voice. "Say, do I know you? Yes, yes, you were dancing like a balloon lady at the last celebration, attracting all kinds of attention with that luscious gold dance outfit you were wearing. I remember you now. If I remember correctly, we never did get the opportunity to share a dance, you and me, together, did we?"

"No," I began, and he interrupted me again.

"Well, my darling," he purred, moving closer to me, "today will be our chance to dance! After you change into your luscious clothing of the celebration and we all meet in the grand room of the celebration, we can dance together, you and I, along with the hundreds of others who will be sharing our dance. We will make up for not dancing together at the last dance, the one under the stars.

"And who do we have here?" he asked, noticing Lena standing beside me. "My sweet little kitten, we have not met before, have we? As a matter of fact, I have never seen you around here. You will be very attractive in a zebra leotard, prancing around the dance floor, tiny as you are, oh, I can just picture you now." He gave her the most disturbing smile, as both of us shrank back into the safety of Nadir's arms.

"These girls are with me," Nadir said protectively.

"Yes, of course they are!" the creepy man said. "And you will all be with us at the celebration! I can hardly wait." He gave a weird little shudder, perhaps of excitement.

"Can you tell me where they take people who are captured?" I asked.

"Captured?" he asked, with an odd look on his face. "People are not captured here, and you ought to know that. Where do you think we are, anyway? In the Evil Sector?"

"What is this Evil Sector?" Nadir asked.

"Ah, yes, wouldn't we all like to know?" the man asked, shaking his head. "We can just all thank the lucky stars that we are living here, in this wonderful community of freedom, instead of in captivity in the Evil Sector."

"No, I mean, where did they take those two men who were taken away from the wedding ceremony?" I asked, trying to keep the conversation on track.

"What two men are you talking about, little darling?" the man asked, with that creepy smile returning to his face.

"The men who interrupted the weddings! They were grabbed and pulled away!" I said, as I began to get frustrated with this man.

"The weddings were not interrupted!" the man exclaimed. "They were performed as planned, and were the brides not so beautiful? This will be a day I will always remember, a day I will never forget, the day of the wonderful union of our two fine princes to the two lovely young ladies."

"But it was interrupted!" I said, stamping my foot.

"Layla," Nadir whispered, "you must calm yourself."

I realized he was right. This goofy man did not know anything useful. We would have to do some investigating, and discover for ourselves where my dad and Uncle Pierce had been taken.

As the end of the line approached the beginning of the crevice, and we were about to enter the long corridor, Lena turned to me.

"What kind of thing is inside of this place?" she asked.

"What do you mean?" I said, not getting what she meant.

"Why we are going into here?" she asked.

"We have not been inside this place," Nadir said.

CHAPTER 12

I stopped, holding them back a little from the rest of the line. We were the final three in line, and I wanted a bit of privacy to be able to talk to them.

"You haven't been in here?" I asked. They shook their heads, looking at me with anticipation. "It is like a city that is built into the walls of the canyon, and I guess everyone lives inside of here. This is the only way in, and they have guards standing up above, up there," I pointed to the ledges, but from here, the guards could not be seen, "so, I guess, no one can sneak in and take them by surprise. Unless they fall from above."

"Fall from above?" Nadir asked. "What you do mean by this expression?"

"Well, if someone jumped out of an airplane or helicopter, they could 'drop in,' or, I suppose, someone could climb down the canyon wall, if they had the right equipment, ropes and stuff, to climb down a wall, I guess they could get in that way."

"You came in this way with your uncle?" Lena asked.

"Well, no," I said, as we moved slowly forward, but keeping my voice very low so no one else could hear me. "We were up above, Uncle Pierce and I, and we met a boy, one of those boys, my brother. He showed us a secret way to get into the palace from up there. And then he showed us how to sneak through the palace, through a secret escape route, and we came out of the palace, at the bottom of the canyon."

"Palace?" Lena asked, a little too loudly. I motioned for her to keep her voice down. "You were inside a real palace?"

Nadir was looking straight up, at the walls of the thin corridor, as we were entering it.

"Do not say anything," he instructed us.

We walked through the long, narrow corridor in silence, following the others until we finally reached the floor of the canyon. We stopped and stared for a moment. From this angle, the natural splendor of the canyon was amazing. I was completely impressed by the way the people had not really altered the natural beauty, but had rather enhanced it with the buildings that had been carved into its walls.

Like before, people were all over the place, moving in every direction; only now, some had changed from their red outfits into flowing gold and silver clothing, giving the entire place a look of elegance and fluid movement. I noticed that lots of people were going in and out of the clothing store where Uncle Pierce and I had gotten our red clothing.

"If you two have not been in here," I said quietly, as Lena and Nadir stood, taking in this magnificent sight and the flurry of activity, "where did you get the red clothes you are wearing?"

"Your friend land the plane way over in that area," Nadir said, waving his hand to our left. "Your father and we all get out of the plane and we see nothing. Your friend tell us your mother is to be found near this area and he point here. He say he must go back to work, and he go back to the plane and take off in the plane.

"We walk over this way and we see all people are gathering here, and all are wearing red clothing. We keep walking and man comes to approach us and tells us we need to change to red clothes. He then gives us the red clothes and we put on red clothing over our clothes. We wait for very long time, standing over to side. Your father beginning to look through the people to try to find your mother, but too many people there, with more coming out from here, and he cannot find her. We stay waiting very long time, until finally ceremony begins. All music and passing of cup and everything happening, we all wait with patience, and he keeps looking for your mother. He is beginning to be upset when wedding does not include holy words of God, so he start walking closer to tell them what is important about wedding. You saw what happened at that time?"

"Yes, but where can he be now?" I asked, suddenly feeling very anxious. "Maybe if we can get up higher, in one of those buildings, we can look out the window and see from up there."

"I would like to remind you, Layla and Lena, keep voice very quiet when by sides of walls, because voice travels up to people listening above," Nadir said, and I understood why he did not want us to speak while we were going through the corridor. The guards up above must have been put up there for a reason, and one reason could be to listen for anything of interest that could be spoken down below by unsuspecting persons.

"I need to find somewhere to change my clothes," I said, leading them toward the clothing store. "I have my clothes in my backpack, but I need a place to change.

"Maybe we are not to put on our own clothing," Lena suggested, as she looked out at all the other people, the natives of this land. "They will know we are not from here."

"Let's go in there," I said. "We can dress in fancy clothes like the others, and we can leave these red clothes in there. Then maybe we can find my dad, or someone who can help us find him."

We slipped into the shop where people were going in wearing red and coming out all dressed up in fancy gold and silver clothing. It seemed to be a type of clothing exchange. Ones were discarding their red items, putting them into giant tubs, after they had put on the elegant clothing. I watched carefully, and did not see anyone paying for anything. They came in wearing red, selected a stylish gold or silver outfit, changed behind the dividing screens, and then left their red clothing in the tubs. We could do that!

Lena and I joined the women in the area where fancy dresses were on display while Nadir disappeared among the men's fashions. Lena was overwhelmed by the selection of clothing, so I helped her find an outfit that was both beautiful and practical. It was silver and sparkly with several short sashes flowing off the sleeves, and the dress was knee-length with enough room to move her legs without them being constricted. She stepped behind the divider and quickly changed from red to silver clothing. Since she was so tiny, the dress fit her perfectly, giving her room to move without being tight or embarrassing her by clinging to her body.

"You have to wear this one!" a lady shouted, shoving a gold dress into my face. "You will look absolutely perfect in it! I believe it was made just for you!"

"Thank you," I mumbled, not really wanting to wear gold, but taking the dress from her and holding it up, looking at it to be polite. The feeling of the fabric was magnificent, smooth and silky, and the gold was both sparkly and reflective, but it was too outlandish for me.

"Put it on, put it on!" the lady begged me.

"I am looking for something a little more--" I began,

thinking that I really wanted it to be a little less.

"Oh, no, you do protest too much!" she shouted, attracting all kinds of attention that I did not want. "What do you think, Mijkin?" she asked loudly.

"My goodness!" a short lady, presumably Mijkin, screamed. "Oh, my young friend, any other dress could never do you justice like this one will!" she said, fanning herself with her hand. "Do you not agree with me, Jabbon?"

I was not sure justice was the look I was going for, and I looked at them doubtfully. "I really would rather wear--"

"Oh, you MUST wear that one!" Jabbon, insisted, as she struggled to pull on a silver dress that looked to be way too small for her. "You will be the belle of the ball, the talk of the town, and I am not kidding when I say that! Oh, just look at you! I am imagining you in that dress, and the only thing that could be any more lovely is when I see you actually wearing that dress!"

My intention was to not attract attention, so I was not looking forward to being the talk of any town; however, now, it seemed, all attention in the place was on me.

I smiled respectfully, as I desperately searched for a more appropriate outfit.

"Come now, come now, you must try it on!" Mijkin said. "Come on, I will help you! You do not have a choice in the matter. You cannot say no!"

"Oh, now, do not be shy!" Jabbon said. "Mijkin and I will help you. You must at least try it on to give us the satisfaction of seeing you in this exquisite creation!"

I gave a look at Lena, a desperate expression of help, but she was just smiling at me as Jabbon and Mijkin forced me behind the divider screen.

"I really don't want to wear this one," I said, as they were stripping the red outfit from my body.

"Oh, nonsense!" Mijkin said. "Do not even think about being self-conscious when you will be wearing the most beautiful gown in the entire community!" She held up the gold dress to examine it, and I saw little golden wings coming off the back of it, two wings on each shoulder that appeared to flap as she moved the dress.

"We will call you our little angel!" Jabbon exclaimed, as she and Mijkin pulled and shoved and pushed the dress onto me. "You will be the jewel of the celebration!"

"I don't really think--" I said, before I was interrupted again.

"Oh, my dear little one, you do not need to waste your precious time thinking!" Mijkin said, as she fastened the buttons on the back of the dress.

"All you have to do is to look beautiful!" Jabbon agreed. "Oh, and smile, of course. Your smile adds a tremendous effect to your beauty."

I was pondering that remark, still looking for a means of escape from this entire scene when the lady who had discovered the dress poked her head behind the screen.

"I simply cannot wait to see – oh, my goodness, oh my, oh my, you look so…" She began to cry, real tears flowing down her cheeks.

"I know, I know!" Mijkin said, as she, too began to sob. "Doesn't she, though, Franchesca Simmbaba?"

"She is just the most!" Jabbon said loudly. "Just look

at her. I almost cannot believe it! My little one, you were made to wear this gown, on this very day, a day like none other!"

After fussing over me, touching my hair, straightening my dress, tugging here and there, they pushed me out from behind the screen.

Jabbon clapped her hands loudly. "Everyone, everyone, I would like to have your attention, please! EXCUUUSE MEEEE! I apologize for interrupting, but I have an announcement to make!"

The noisy buzz of the place was instantly quiet as hundreds of people, popping out from behind racks and shelves, turned to face us. I was hoping this would be the instant that I would awaken from this embarrassing nightmare, fearing that the dress had disappeared and I was standing there, exposed; but, no, I could not get out of this situation that easily. I was still standing there, exposed, in this hideous creation, and everyone in the room was looking in my direction.

"I am happy to announce…" she began, and with her announcement of happiness, Mijkin and Franchesca Simmbaba burst into tears, wailing loudly, "that we have an angel among us. Come, look, feast your eyes on this delicacy, and you will be ready to leave this earth and step into heaven, after your eyes have seen the most glorious sight."

At this point, I could feel my face turning the darkest possible shade of red, as if it were sticking out several inches, and fiery hot. I wanted to pull my entire head and neck into the dress, the way a turtle retracted his head into his shell. I was definitely going to be the belle of the ball, all right.

"My little dear, give us a show!" Mijkin said, in between her exaggerated sobs. "Come on, step and turn! Let us all see the beautiful gown, and how you were made to wear it on this special occasion! We are all eager to see and enjoy your beauty and grace! Move back, move back, give the young lady some space to display this magnificent creation!"

The circle around us widened a bit, and, since I was frozen in my tracks, unwilling to even take one step, someone gave me just a little shove from behind. Surprised and off-balance, my head flew back on my rubbery neck as my left foot jabbed forward involuntarily, and I stumbled several steps, about as ungraceful as I could possibly be. I could hear a slight snicker from Lena, and I was sure she didn't mean it, but the rest of the crowd oohed and aahed, as if I were the loveliest creature in the world. I caught myself before I did a complete tumble, and I fell against a shelf full of stacks of clothing, sending a flash of golden-colored scarves flying like a flock of delicate birds onto the gathered mob, as I wanted nothing more than to ditch the dress, put on comfortable work clothes, and run out of this place.

The entire place erupted in applause as I blinked back tears of shame.

"Now, you see?" Jabbon said. "Do you not all agree that this is a creation straight from heaven itself?"

"Oh, our little angel is so touched by the beauty and by the compassion you are showing her, even she is crying," Franchesca Simmbaba announced, as she put her arm around me and continued to weep openly. "We will all have a glorious time at the celebration!" she managed to say, before completely breaking down and crying. Jabbon wrapped her fleshy arms around Franchesca Simmbaba and patted her back to comfort her.

A very pretty man with his black hair slicked to his head leaped over to me and lifted the gown off the floor, just enough to see my feet, the same feet that had been wearing hiking boots for the previous few days.

"Oh!" he shrieked, directing the attention of everyone to my feet. "These will never do! You must not dishonor this gown, this creation of magnificence with these… these… oh, I surely cannot dignify these things with a name! Vendome, Darling! Can you get a pair of golden float slippers over here? And I mean, right now! It looks like she wears a size two, so I'm sure she will fit into a size three, but since a size four will be more comfortable for her, maybe you should bring me a size five."

He looked up at me. "You may be an angel, but not with these things on those feet. Brace yourself! I am going to remove these awful, clunky things and toss them away where they will never disgrace another pair of angelic feet again!"

Another man who also had black hair slicked to his head squeezed through the crowd carrying a pair of gold shoes that looked like little silky tubes.

"Here you are, Shaktome," he said to the guy who was untying my shoes and removing them with a dramatic flair.

"Thank you, Vendome," Shaktome said. He sat on the floor in front of me so he could have better access to my feet. When he was finally able to get the boots off my feet, while I was standing on one foot and then the other, he wiped each foot delicately with a small towel.

He pulled some silky stockings out of his pocket and slipped them on my feet, pulling them up to my knees. He took the shoes from Vendome, holding them as if they were the lost treasures of the world, and gently slid one onto my foot. He then held up my foot to display it to the audience, who applauded enthusiastically, as I held my hands out to my sides to keep from losing my balance. He set my foot with the golden shoe very carefully on the floor as he turned his attention to the other foot. After he had both shoes in place, he stepped back, holding my gown above my ankles so everyone could see what they were heralding as the sight of the year: golden slippers on my feet. As I glanced down at them, I was horrified to see the shoes were beginning to glow, from golden to bright yellow and back to golden again, making my feet appear to grow and shrink with the light.

"Oh, my, those are lovely!" someone shouted.

"I have never seen such beauty!" a woman exclaimed, drawing her hands up to her mouth.

"Golden slippers on heavenly feet!" another lady said, sucking in her breath.

"What a sight for our humble eyes to behold!"

"Her feet are dancing in those lovely shoes and they are not even moving!"

"I wish I could capture this sight and save it to take it with me wherever I go!"

"Those feet! Those shoes! What a sight!"

Several people fell to their knees to be able to get a better look at the slippers on my feet while others continued to make ridiculous comments about them. I kept a fake smile on my face to keep myself from saying something unkind to these people, who were not really doing anything wrong, they were just all acting like they were crazy.

Shaktome and Vendome let my dress fall gently to the floor and they both took a bow, as they nodded to their audience. After an extended applause, everyone went back to what they were doing before my moment of embarrassment. I turned to Franchesca Simmbaba.

"Do I have to wear this now?" I asked her quietly, devising a plan in my mind, to first change into something discreet and then quietly slip out of here. "Can I put on something else now, something less grand, and change into this dress later?"

"Oh, no, oh, no, you simply cannot entertain that idea," she answered, shaking her head violently. "The celebration is about to begin, and you must walk into it wearing this angelic gown, so everyone can experience the glorious sight of you, entering the palace ballroom, donning this magnificent golden creation. Even the princes and the Queen will be amazed and impressed when they see you gracing the celebration with your angelic beauty."

I was about to voice my objection when a new plan began to form in my mind. Wouldn't the two brides – my mom and Aunt Moon – be with the princes at the celebration? That is, if my mom had recovered from her faint. Perhaps this outrageous outfit was my ticket to the grand ball, and my opportunity to meet up with my mother, before she was locked away and unreachable in the palace.

Lena came over to me, trying to stifle a giggle. I winked at her and her expression suddenly grew grave.

"What you are thinking?" she asked, very quietly,

under her breath.

I smiled at her graciously, in case others were watching us. "We are going to attend the celebration," I said.

CHAPTER 13

Lena and I calmly blended into the swarm of people as they were leaving the shop, heading toward the celebration at the palace. She looked at me anxiously, so I tried to still her fears.

"Apparently, everyone will be at this celebration," I said, as we were moved along with the flow of people toward the palace.

She looked at me, not comprehending my meaning.

"You know, everyone," I said, "including the princes and the brides and the sons, and everyone else."

"Your father will be there?" she asked, missing the point, but bringing up one I had not considered.

"Maybe he will be there, and Uncle Pierce, too!" I said. This celebration could be where my whole family would get together!

As we began to approach the grand entryway to the palace, an enormous arch of gold, finely carved with delicate designs, we were swept away, under the wings of a giant woman who was wearing a silver gown with sashes flying off of it in all directions.

"Darlings, Darlings!" she said, swooping each of us under an arm. "You simply cannot go into the celebration looking like that!"

"What you do mean?" Lena asked, looking up at her.

I shrugged, thinking that we looked better than we ever had in our lives. After all, just a week or so ago, Lena's wardrobe consisted of a few robes with hoods, and my clothing ranged from useful work clothes to useful sleepers. Now we were wearing silky, flowing, dazzling dresses that were not actually a color, but Lena's was sparkling silver and mine was glittering gold. It was safe to say we had never looked so fine before.

"I do mean, my little Sweetie," she said, with a kind of sing-songy voice, "you must have your hair done before you can go into the palace for the celebration."

"Oh, you have hair managers here?" I asked, trying to remember the last time my hair had been properly managed.

"Hair managers!" she said distastefully. "We have nothing of the sort! Why would you degrade our artistic community by saying that?"

"I don't know," I replied, unsure why she was making such a fuss.

"We have artistic stylists, and I am ashamed of you for disrespecting them so!" she said.

"I am sorry if I offended you," I said.

"I am not offended" she huffed. "However, you need to show due respect to the artistic stylist so that he or she will not make a mistake on your hair."

"A mistake on your hair?" Lena repeated. "What is this kind of mistake?"

The lady laughed. "I have seen some very hilarious results when the owner of the hair did not show due respect to the artistic stylist." Her eyes danced, as she must have been recalling those hilarious results. "Your hair will be absolutely beautiful when they are finished with you," she promised.

"What they will do to my hair?" Lena asked fearfully. I realized that she had never had her long, beautiful hair managed by a professional. Persons who lived in a small tribe in a tent in the middle of the desert did not have access to the same things as people who lived in larger, civilized communities.

"Relax, my little Sweetie!" the lady said, as she squeezed us close to her. "They won't do anything you don't want them to do to your hair. You just tell them what you want and they will do it, only better, much better than you can even imagine, my little Sweetie, because, after all, they are the artistic experts."

"I do not want to do something to my hair," Lena protested. "My hair will stay as it is."

She had no opportunity to look in a mirror, so she could not know that her hair was sticking out all over from the long, beautiful braid it had been a couple of days ago when Salwa had braided it. I could imagine what mine must look like, with my curls going wild, uncombed and untamed.

"Lena, this will be good," I said, leaning around the lady to speak to my friend. "You will like it. It won't hurt, and they will make it look really nice."

She looked at me doubtfully, as we arrived in front of another shop, this one with a large window, painted with beautiful designs so it was difficult to see inside the shop.

"Here we are!" the lady announced.

"I will go first, so you can see what they do," I said to Lena.

"No waiting, you can both go at the same time!" the lady said, ushering us through the door.

"Hashmik! Shambok! I have two young ladies who are in desperate need of your services, right away!" she shouted, among a scurry of activity.

The scent inside this place was overpowering, and Lena slapped her hand across her mouth and nose. My eyes began to burn from the multitude of strong odors that were coming at us from all directions. I squinted to try to see what was happening in here, where the sounds of hundreds of people chattering and water flowing were bombarding my ears. I felt like I was on a sensory overload: bright lights, loud sounds, and strong smells, attacking us as soon as we entered. I could not imagine how terrible it must have been for Lena, who had never experienced anything remotely like this.

"Welcome, welcome!" a high voice screeched at us. "And what do we have here? Oh, yes, two exquisite specimens who require artistic hair services, of course! We will give you the most stylish hair to match those lovely gowns. And do not you worry one bit: you can keep wearing those gorgeous gowns, as we work around them. We will not touch them, nor will we allow any of our chemicals to splash upon them. There is no need for you to remove your gowns!" He or she laughed. (I could not tell who was speaking to us, since my eyes were nearly closed to protect against the irritants in the air.)

Two hands closed gently on my shoulders and guided me to a chair, where I was then seated. My head was pushed back, so my face was toward the ceiling, and the entire chair began to lean backwards. A warm towel was placed on my face, covering my entire face, even my ears, and with my eyes now closed and the sounds and scents muffled, I began to relax. This was familiar to me; we had similar experiences back at the Complex. Although here, they seemed to really be enjoying themselves rather than merely existing in a utilitarian society, the way Complex-dwellers did.

"No, stop!" Lena shouted. "Do not touch my hair! I cannot see what you are doing to me! Do not touch my hair!"

"My little Sweetie, you are in careful hands," the lady told her. "They will wash it and style it in a fashion that will be so beautiful, you will not even recognize yourself."

"I do not know if that will be good for me or bad for me?" Lena asked.

I could almost imagine Lena's apprehension at this unusual ritual, but I was really beginning to enjoy the gentle massaging of my head. I felt the nice, warm water being poured over my scalp as tender finger pads made small circles all over my head. I could have fallen asleep – as a matter of fact, I think I did fall asleep for a few minutes, while my head was put into a state of complete unwind. The tension that had built up from the time of the wedding and losing track of my parents to the awful scene where I had been made a spectacle in a golden gown was flowing away from my mind, being washed away from my head, and I was feeling very peaceful.

Time passed, but I had no idea if we had been in there for five minutes or five hours when my chair was returned to an upright position and the warm towel was removed from my face. I felt light-headed and dizzy, as if waking from a long winter's nap. I realized that I had not heard Lena speak in quite some time, then it dawned on me: I had been sedated. The towels must have had some kind of substance in them that made us relax, or even go to sleep. I was so groggy as I struggled to open my eyes.

My chair was whirled around so I was facing a

young lady in a silly golden dress. Her face was puffy and dark red, and her eyes looked like little slits carved in stone. She had golden hair that was the exact same color as her dress. Her hair was styled in the most preposterous way, pointing this direction and that, a big bubble of a hairstyle that looked like some huge, strange kind of helmet with out-of-control spiky points. I didn't want to laugh, but she was smiling at me. I tried to keep a straight face, but her grin was widening, and we both broke into an extreme fit of laughter at the same time. I was laughing so hard, I felt tears begin to come to my eyes. The other girl was laughing just as hard as I was, and I began to wonder if my hair looked as bad as hers did. I began to lift my hand to touch my hair, to see if I could feel my own hairstyle. She mimicked me, raising her hand as well.

I suddenly stopped laughing when I realized I was looking at myself in a mirror! That awful, crazy hairdo was on my own head! If these were hairstyle artists, they had taken art to the utmost degree. I shook my head a little, in an attempt to make my hair look even the slightest bit natural and was shocked to see that when I moved my head, my hair did not move!

"What have you done to my hair?" I tried to say, but my voice came out muffled, a mere, "Waha-u-duh-duh-ma-ha?" My tongue was thick in my mouth, and in the mirror I could see that my lips were all puffed up like the lips of one of the Before Time painted clowns.

"Oh, yes!" a voice squealed. "Now you can go to the grand celebration! You will be able to make a grand entry in your grand, golden gown and your grand artistic hairstyle! I can tell you right here and now, you will be the talk of the celebration! Oh, my dear, if I could only walk in beside you and get a first-hand look at the expression on the faces of the royal family, I would simply die!"

I felt like I was going to simply die of embarrassment, right at that very moment. Was the helmet-hair removable? Could I leave it here and get my own hair back again?

The lady who had brought us into this place turned my chair so I was no longer facing the mirror, so I could see the huge group of people who were in here, either having their hair disfigured or watching someone else be made into a laughingstock. The lady clapped her hands loudly as I tried to shrink into my hair and dress, so my face could not be seen.

"I would like to have your attention, right over here, right now!" she shouted, as she waved her arms above her head, so no one could miss her. "Yoo-hoo, everyone, I am talking to you!" As soon as about two hundred sets of eyes were focused on me with my golden fiasco, she continued. "Shambok and Hashmik have done it again! Feast your eyes on this never-before-seen artistic creation!"

"My goodness! Shambok and Hashmik are true artists who have no equal!" someone commented. Two men with pasty faces took a bow, so I assumed they were Shambok and Hashmik.

"Oh, that hair, I love that hair!" said a young girl who must have been about fourteen years old. "When I get old like her, I want to have hair just like that!"

Now the insults were obviously not to be contained to my absurd hair, but to my old age of seventeen as well.

"You hair is beauty to behold," an older lady said

kindly, reminding me of an old saying that beauty was in the eye of the beholder. In this case, nothing could be more true.

"I just want to eat it up!" another lady said, as she stepped out of the crowd to move closer to me.

"Adirolf, you keep your mouth away from our creation!" Shambok or Hashmik said teasingly. "I know what kind of an appetite you have, you naughty girl, and you would not leave it looking like anything at all!"

"But, Shambok, her hair is the picture of perfection!" the lady pouted.

"And we want it to stay that way," Shambok said. He moved near to me and very lightly touched my hair.

The onlookers gave a collective gasp, so I glanced back at the mirror. My hair was glowing! Tiny lights had come on, all over the helmet-hair so my entire head was all lit up!

"We don't do this for just anyone," Shambok confided in me, as he leaned down to tell me in my ear. "But when we saw what we had to work with, well, what else could we do? We took one look at your hair and we felt just like the potter when he has the perfect lump of clay, and he can take it, and he can punch it, and he can pull it, and he can squash it, and he can round it, and he can smooth it, and he can mold it into that unique bowl or cup or vase, and he can paint it and he can glaze it and he can fire it and he can form it into a thing of beauty that will last forever."

"Forever, yes, forever, to be sure; or at least until someone drops it and breaks it and it shatters into several thousand pieces, my darling," Hashmik said with a deep-throated laugh.

Shambok and Hashmik giggled for a moment before growing serious again.

"We do not have to worry about you dropping your hair and having it shatter into several thousand pieces, now, do we, my precious one?" Shambok said, looking right into my eyes.

I was afraid to try to speak, so I subtly shook my head.

"Are you ready to go to the celebration, my young one?" the lady who brought us here asked, as the crowd began to disperse and I was no longer the unwilling center of attention.

"Where is Lena?" I managed to ask, speaking slowly and deliberately. I was suddenly afraid for her – what if her hair looked even half as bad as mine did?

"What are you saying, my precious one?" Shambok said, leaning down so his face was about two inches from mine. "Do you need something? What can I get for you? Are you feeling thirsty? Oh, I want to let you know, you must be aware, and I do not believe we have mentioned this fact to you yet, but you will need to use a straw for drinking until your lips return to their natural state, a couple of days from now."

"Two days?" I said, trying to clear my head of its fogginess.

"Well, it could be two days, or it could be three, or most likely they will stay like this for four or five days, but we can never be sure, since everyone's lips react differently," Hashmik said. "You know, I remember one lady, do you remember, my dear Shambok, the one lady with the very sensitive lips? Her lips stayed like this for almost twenty-four days! Oh, she was so happy. We cannot promise that you will be so lucky as she was. It will most likely wear off within six or seven days, probably not more than ten days."

"Stay like this for ten days?" I asked. Why was this situation getting worse by the moment?

"You can only hope, my precious one," Shambok said. "You can only hope."

"Where is my friend?" I asked, remembering what my question had been in the first place.

"Which friend is that, of whom you speak?" Shambok asked.

"She came with me," I said, forcing my tongue to cooperate with my brain.

"Where did she come with you?" Shambok said, shaking his head, as if he couldn't understand me.

"Here! She came here with me, when I came in!" I said.

"My precious one, you have no reason to shout," Hashmik said gently, as he moved his hands in a pressing-down motion to lower my voice.

"My friend, Lena, came with me here, when I came, just a while ago," I said, using extreme care to control my voice.

"Oh, did she?" Shambok asked. "I am afraid I did not notice who accompanied you here. Oh, I take that back. I apologize for my mistake. I did notice Farcheesy, and she is still standing right beside you."

I turned to Farcheesy, the lady who had brought us here, who was right beside me, but by the look on her face, her mind was on another planet. "Where is Lena? The other girl who came in here with us, where is she now?"

Farcheesy laughed with deep passion as her eyes focused on me. I wasn't sure if it was because of my insane hairstyle or if she was simply crazy.

"You are a handful, are you not?" she asked, tilting her head to the side as she examined my face. "You will have a wonderful time at the celebration in the palace. We really should be going over there right about now, don't you know, so we won't miss the opening ceremonies and all the fun that goes along with those rituals. Oh, no, we definitely do not want to miss any of that, now, do we? No, of course not, of course, we do not."

"Where is Lena, my friend that was with me when you brought us over here?" I repeated, trying to make my voice sound stern.

"You have absolutely no reason to worry," Shambok said, patting my shoulder daintily. "Everything is going to work out just fine for you. You should be sitting here with the most confidence of anyone in this entire community, don't you know? Get rid of those negative thoughts! Let them go! Be gone! Be gone, you thoughts of negativity! Go on, get out of here, and do not come back to bother this lovely, precious one again!" He began to use his hands to wave away what he perceived to be negative thoughts, to shoo them away from my head. "You have no place in this lovely head!"

He changed the motion of his hands to scoop air towards my head. "Now, I call out to you, I summon you, thoughts of joy, thoughts of peace, thoughts of positive experience! Come in! Come on, now, right in here! Come in and make your abode inside the head of this young woman! Thoughts of good things and happy futures, come right on in here, and manifest yourself right here, in this darling little head!"

He stopped the crazy motions and looked at me sincerely. "Now, tell me right now, do you or do you not feel one hundred percent or maybe even two hundred percent better, with these positive notions inside your head and those others, which I do not care to mention for fear of validating them, out of there forever?"

I smiled at him to project the positive notions towards him. "I just want to know, where is my friend, Lena?"

"Oh, a curious one, you are," Hashmik said, returning my smile. "I perceive that you have always had a curious mind and you have always been a girl who asked a lot of questions. Why, just now, we have only just met, and we have heard you ask several questions already, little Miss Curious. Tell me, can you remember what was the first question you ever asked? I mean, as a child, when you were just a tiny tot, what was your first question? You were a curious child, were you not? You can tell me. You have no reason to be ashamed."

"I don't see--" I began, before the two kooks cut me off again.

"Are your eyes okay? Do they hurt? Did you get something in them?" Shambok asked, his face filling with concern. He bent down and began to examine my eyes closely.

"You are not able to see back that far in your life?" Hashmik asked. "Oh, come on, for me, try, try, try to remember! I would love nothing more than to know what was the first question you ever asked as a curious little child! Think! Think back! If you would like, I can help to put you in a state of relaxation so that you will be able to remember as far back as that first question."

"Where is my friend?" I repeated, wondering what it would take for them to actually listen to what I was saying.

"Oh!" Hashmik squealed. "I never would have guessed! What an unusual child you must have been! But, really, it is no wonder, because look at what an unusual young lady you have turned out to be. Yes, yes, I can understand how you would begin your life of curiosity with that question. Yes, yes, it is all beginning to make sense now." He was nodding his head as if he had just solved the world's greatest riddle.

I turned again to Farcheesy. "Can we get my friend, Lena, and get out of here?" I asked.

"Now, now, you have no reason to act in a rude manner, nor do you have reason to be ungrateful to these champion artistic stylists," Farcheesy said, scolding me. "Just look at what they have done for you, and you can be more than thankful to them, not only today, but for the rest of your life."

"Yeah, yeah, I am thankful and I am grateful, but you were saying that we should get going so we won't miss the opening ceremonies of the celebration?" I said to her, in the most heartfelt voice I could muster.

"Oh, yes, I know I heard that somewhere," she said absent-mindedly. "Did you come here with a friend?" she asked.

"Yes! Yes! Lena came with us!" I exclaimed, amazed that she had finally made the connection. "Where is she? Is she ready to go with us?"

"I suppose we can find her, and then we can ask her if she is ready to go," Farcheesy said, as if it were all her idea.

"Yes, good thinking," I said, in an attempt to encourage her.

"Well, then, what are we waiting for? Why are we standing here discussing it when we can be looking for her?" she asked, looking at me for the answers.

"I was just wondering the same thing," I said, nodding in agreement.

"Well, it is nice to know that we are in the same frame of mind, and we are not going off in different directions," she said.

"Shambok, Hashmik, can you help our young friend get out of this chair?" Farcheesy asked.

"Oh, yes, we are so sorry, Madame," Shambok said, as the two of them awkwardly moved about until they could help me climb ungracefully out of the chair.

Farcheesy took my arm.

"You take care of that masterpiece hair, my little precious one," Shambok said.

"Be careful at the end of the day when it will be time to pull your gown over your head," Hashmik warned. "Whatever you do, you will not want to break your hair."

I had to stifle a laugh. "Okay, I will," I promised.

"You will break it?" Hashmik asked, with a look of panic on his face.

"No, I meant I will be careful," I clarified.

"Oh, you just about caused my heart to stop," Hashmik said dramatically. I had a feeling his entire life was pretty dramatic.

"Thank you both, so much, for all you have done for

me," I said, trying to get into the swing of things in this strange place.

Shambok and Hashmik beamed at me as Farcheesy guided me away from them. Although I did not dare to look back at them, I thought I heard them crying as we left.

"We will look for your friend," Farcheesy said, her enthusiasm renewed. "She must be in here somewhere, don't you think? Or do you think she left us to go to the celebration when her hair was ready?"

"No, I am sure she is still here," I said. "She would not leave me here and go over there alone."

The place was enormous, and we began to check each station as we passed, looking for Lena.

"I heard her earlier, and I think she was pretty close to me," I said.

"Oh, no, her hair was very long," Farcheesy said.

"Her hair WAS long?" I asked, as my heart skipped a beat. "Are you saying that you think they cut it?"

"Oh, no, of course not," Farcheesy said, with a little laugh. "I am not saying that at all. They would have to take her, along with her long hair, to the back in order to take care of it properly. What do you think, that they can take care of long hair at just any artistic hair styling station? They must go to the back to care for long hair! My silly little angel!"

"So, let's go to the back," I said, pulling a bit in that direction.

"Yet, when they finished, that is, if they have already finished, she would be brought back to the front, in which case she would not be in the back, but she would be in the front, unless they are not yet finished with her. In that case, she would still be in the back," Farcheesy said. This new piece of information was not at all helpful.

"You are saying she might be in the back and she might not be in the back?" I asked.

"When you put it that way, yes," Farcheesy said, nodding, "that is what I am saying. She might be in the back, but she just as well might not be in the back. I do suppose that the only way to find out where she is would be to find out where she is."

My frustration level with this woman was boiling over, but at this point, I could not do a thing about it. I decided to just keep looking for Lena and stop talking.

"Oh, dear, oh, dear," Farcheesy moaned, "where, oh where can she be? What is the name you have given her? Perhaps we can call out her name and she will respond, that is, if she hears us calling her name. If she does not hear us, she will not be able to respond to our call."

"Her name is Lena, but I didn't give it to her," I said, immediately regretting that I had added this unnecessary detail. Farcheesy's attention span was about half a second long, and I knew I had just pointed her in the wrong direction.

Farcheesy stopped in her tracks and put her hand on my shoulder, turning me to face her. "If you did not give her this name, where did she get it? Who gave it to her? How can she go around with you, using a name you did not give to her?"

"I am pretty sure her parents gave her this name when she was born," I said, trying to get her to keep going, to get back to our search for Lena.

Farcheesy refused to move. "You do know that is against the rules of this community, don't you?"

I stared at her, not even wanting to attempt to guess what she was talking about.

"Oh, I do beg you to please forgive me," she said, her face softening. "You will forgive me, will you not? I simply would not be able to live with myself for even one short second if you do not tell me you will forgive me! Please, I am begging you, please forgive me!"

"Yes, of course," I said, smiling at her, without having any idea why I was forgiving her. "You are forgiven."

"I thank you, I thank you, I sincerely thank you!" she exclaimed, clapping her hands with swift, tiny claps. "I am so sure that you have no idea how much this means to me," she said dramatically.

"No, I don't," I agreed, only wanting to get back to the business of finding Lena. I kept looking into each hair styling station as we were passing by them, but so far, she was not in any of them. The back of the room was quite a distance away from us, and I was hoping we would not be spending the next hour searching the entire room.

"You are such a precious one," Farcheesy said, causing me to begin to dislike that expression.

"Layla!" Lena's voice called out to me from the next station, as we were approaching it. I was not able to see her from where we were, but I was so relieved.

"There she is!" I cried with excitement to Farcheesy. I hurried to see Lena, hoping her hairstyle was not as bizarre as mine was.

"This is my friend, and I like to go with her now," Lena was saying to two men who were hovering over her. She was strapped into a chair that was reclined so far back that her feet were at a higher level than her head, which I still was unable to see.

"With long and beautiful hair like yours, you must learn to have an extreme amount of patience," one man was telling her. "These things take time, little one. We can never rush when caring for hair of this quality and quantity. At the proper time, we will release you, but we are unable to do it prematurely, for the risk of unfortunate consequences. You must be patient and wait. You may not tell us when you are ready to leave, for you do not know the proper process and procedure and the timing that is required."

"He is telling the truth, you know," the other man added. "You have no reason to disbelieve him, especially not at a time like this."

"I like to go with my friend now," Lena repeated, and I could hear a note of anxiety in her voice.

"Oh, well, why did you not just say so in the first place?" the first man said, completely contradicting everything they had just told her. "We can get you ready to go right now, if you like."

"Yes, I do like," she said.

Farcheesy and I got as close to Lena as we could. I couldn't wait to see what they had done to her hair.

One of the men pulled a lever on the chair, and the two of them gently pulled the back of the chair into an upright position. Lena's hair and face had towels covering them, and I became aware that I was holding my breath in anticipation as they very slowly removed the towels. They each held one side of the towel on Lena's face and lifted it gently, as if it were going to break. When it was no longer touching her face, one man took the towel and placed it on a table behind him. I looked closely to see if her face had been changed to sunset orange to burnt sienna like mine had, but, no, her face was the same color as it had been before we came to this house of irrationality. Her lips had not been transformed into clown lips. As a matter of fact, her natural beauty was glowing, subtly enhanced, and she did not look like any kind of ridiculous creature.

She began squinting her eyes against the bright lights, the same way I had been doing, as the two men moved to grasp the towel that was covering her hair. They kind of swirled the towel around and pulled it up, revealing the most beautiful hair I had ever seen: several thick braids that were twisted around her head in a very flattering pattern. Lena looked so elegant and sophisticated, I almost didn't recognize her.

She looked right through me, her eyes searching until they finally rested on Farcheesy. "I hear the voice of Layla. Where she is now?"

"Why, my little Darling," Farcheesy cooed, "the young lady that you call Layla is standing right here beside me! Isn't she just the most stunning creation you have ever seen in your life?"

Lena looked at me with astonishment, blinking her eyes again and again. "This person is Layla? What this word does mean, 'stunning,' you say?"

Farcheesy bellowed and I felt like dying. Lena kept looking at me, trying to find the real me somewhere in all that 'stunning' mess.

"Yes, it's me," I confessed. "How do you like it?"

"I do not know it is you!" she said, struggling to get out of the chair.

"Wait a moment, my child!" the man standing to her right said. "We need to disconnect your snaps."

"I do not have a snaps!" Lena said, her face scrunching up with worry. "I must see my face in murur."

I smiled uncomfortably, thinking that she must be worried that these men had made her look as 'stunning' as Shambok and Hashmik had made me.

"You look beautiful, Lena," I reassured her.

"I do look stunning like you?" she asked.

"No," I said, at the same time as Farcheesy was saying, "Yes!"

"You look beautiful, but you do not look at all like I do," I said, with an emphasis on 'not.'

The two men disconnected Lena from the chair so she was able to stand and join Farcheesy and me.

"You will both amaze and transfix all who see you today in the palace," one of the men predicted, looking Lena up and down.

"When I see you over there later," the other man said to her, "I will ask you for the greatest honor: one dance, just one dance with you."

"I do not know--" she began.

"Of course she will dance with you, Lechbak," Farcheesy said, "but just one dance! Come, now, girls, we don't want to be late!"

Lechbak jumped up and down a few times in anticipation as Farcheesy latched her hands in our arms and guided Lena and me out of that shop of lunacy. As we finally emerged, I breathed in the fresh air deeply, grateful to be pulling it into my lungs, before I began to act as foolish as all those people inside who had obviously inhaled too many noxious fumes.

"Hurry up, girls, we want to make a noticeable entrance!" Farcheesy said, pulling us through the crowd toward the palace.

From this angle, we had a great view of the splendor and grandeur of the palace: the large windows trimmed with gold, the golden balconies high above the ground, the enormous majestic doorway in the center, which was now packed with people who were lined up, waiting to enter. All of this was embedded within the wall of the canyon. The layers of rock, with the multiple shades of red, orange, brown and yellow, gave a natural beauty with horizontal stripes of color to the entire place.

"I will be able to hold my head high, with the two of you on my arms," Farcheesy said proudly, as if we were her own creations. She was wearing a knee-length chunky silver dress that made me think of foil wrapped around a turkey and giant silver shoes that looked like little boats, so the three of us really made a spectacle. However, everyone in this entire community was now dressed in overstated silver or gold clothing, so we all could have been used as decorations on a giant Christmas tree like the ones we had in the Before Time. I was feeling particularly like a huge golden bell; or could I have been a ding dong?

"Now, young ladies, when we are presented to the Queen, you let me do all the talking," Farcheesy instructed. "I knew her before she became the Queen, so you two don't have to worry about a thing. I know exactly what to say, when to say it, and how to say it, so as not to offend her, or to push any of her buttons – and, boy, you can say that again, does she ever have buttons!"

"What are these buttons?" Lena asked, as Farcheesy tried to squeeze us through the pack of people who had been waiting to enter the palace long before we arrived.

"Oh, my little one, this is exactly what I am saying!" Farcheesy said, yanking on my arm so that I nearly toppled to the ground.

"You are talking buttons?" Lena asked. I really felt sorry for her, because I could not even follow Farcheesy's train of thought, and English was my native language.

"What I am trying to say in the most delicate manner," Farcheesy said, lowering her voice, "is for you two to keep your mouths shut so that you will not say the wrong thing. You do not need to speak. I know how to speak to royalty, since I could have been born into royalty, if I only had been born into the royal family. I have everything under control, and the two of you, as lovely as you are, do not need to say a word. If the Queen should happen to ask either of you a question, and I know that is a very big 'if,' since she most likely will not ask you anything, unless she decides to ask you something, you look to me before speaking, and I will indicate to you whether or not you should speak and answer the question, or if I will be answering the question for you. After all, I do have all the answers, so, really, there is no question that you should be answering; that is, unless I indicate that you should be answering a question, which is not likely at all."

"I am not understanding you," Lena said, with an overtone of frustration in her voice.

"How can I say this?" Farcheesy asked, looking up to the sky for an answer. "When we are presented to the Queen, I will do the talking for us, for myself, and for each of you. You do not speak. But if I want you to speak, I will indicate that I want you to speak, and in that case, you can speak, that is, if you know the answer to the question that the Queen may ask."

"You will indicate this how?" Lena asked.

"Let me make it very simple," Farcheesy said finally. "I will do all the talking, and you two just smile and look around the palace. After all, you have never been in the palace before, and I have."

"Layla was in palace today," Lena said.

I gave her a look that said for her to not say anything about it, but she did not get the hint. She was just looking at Farcheesy defiantly, while I had just accepted Farcheesy's rudeness as an aspect of her personality, necessary for survival in this oddest of all communities.

Farcheesy stopped walking and several people bumped into us.

"You were in the palace today?" she asked me, looking right into my burnt-red puffy face. "Oh, what a kidder you are!" she said with an explosive laugh to Lena, when I did not immediately respond. "You have a little sense of humor! Awww, you are so cute! Everyone knows that no one has been inside the palace today, not earlier, I mean. We were all on the outside today. Today is the great day of celebration, a day like none other!"

I just smiled, keeping my mouth shut as per her instructions, only going along with this whole charade while dressed like a fool because this could be my best opportunity to be in the same place as my mother. After today, I might not have another chance to get in the palace, and my mother could end up being married to one of those princes. I could not let that happen! I had to see my mother and get her out of there today! My heart hurt just thinking about how close I was to her, yet with such a barrier between us!

We slowly moved forward with the group until we were just about to the large, grand entryway. The chatter in this area was considerably more quiet than had been just a few steps back, and I thought about what Nadir had said about voices traveling upward. I looked straight up, over our heads, to one of the balconies, and I noticed that someone was spying on me: one of the twin boys that I now knew was my brother. As soon he saw that I was looking up at him, he disappeared into one of the rooms on the third floor.

Where had Nadir gone? We had lost him in the clothing shop, when this ridiculous outfit had been forced on me! During the whirlwind of activity, we had become separated!

Lena must have made the realization at the same time as I did. "Where Nadir did go?" she asked me quietly, with a frightened look in her eyes.

I did not want to cause her to panic, and neither did I want to panic, so I made myself believe as I was speaking. "We will find him when we get inside. Everyone will be at the celebration, so we will be able to find him there. He is so tall, we will spot him – if he doesn't see us first."

"I do not want to spot him," Lena cried. "I want to find him."

I laughed, relieving the bit of tension I was feeling. "When I said we will spot him, I meant that we will see him."

"Girls, girls!" Farcheesy said sternly. "You must keep your voices down. No, I take that back. You must not speak. We are about to enter the palace!"

Lena looked to me for clarification, but I could only shrug my shoulders, since I had no idea what kind of irrational rules and customs they had in this community.

We silently stepped inside the palace, and I was overcome by its beauty and elegance. The inside of the walls were painted so intricately with beautiful designs and patterns, in bright regal colors. The striking shades of purple and turquoise were complimented with gold and silver. It was obvious that someone had spent a considerable amount of time painting and decorating. I had to concentrate to keep my focus on our mission here, because I could have been so easily distracted by the splendor of the palace. I was curious as to what other rooms were on this floor, off to our left and right, but I didn't have a chance to really see inside of them.

The mob of people was moving upwards. At first, I thought we were being guided to a large curving staircase wide enough for at least ten people to stand side-by-side that was leading to the second floor, but as we got close to it, I could see that it was actually a very large ramp, not stairs. It was made of stone, a natural incline from one floor to the next with a carved wooden railing attached to the outer side of the curve. The inner side was protected by the wall, so no railing was needed on that side. A thought flashed through my mind that those little boys – my brothers and cousin – probably did have quite a lot of fun playing in here. Then I remembered that my task here, to put our family back together again, would result in removing the boys from the palace. So, they would not be having that kind of fun any more; not here, anyway.

As we approached the second floor, I was taken

aback by the sheer size of the room, tall, wide and long. The room must have taken up the entire second floor of this palace. Hundreds of people were moving around this grand ballroom, and I had to remind myself that we were actually inside a cave or cavern that had been carved into the side of the canyon and not in a real palace across the ocean, in some royal kingdom of long ago. Lena grabbed onto my arm as we both gazed at the enormity, the grandeur, and the buzz of activity. I put my hand on top of hers, clinging together, so we would not drown in this sea of hustle and bustle.

Farcheesy stopped to talk to someone she knew, stepping out of the lane that was moving toward a brightly lit area at the far end of the room. Lena and I did not follow her, instead holding our place in the group. I kept standing on my tippy-toes to look for Nadir and my dad and Uncle Pierce, but because of the huge crowd and everyone being dressed in the same colors of silver and gold, along with huge hats and long, flowing scarves and sashes that were blocking my view, I was unable to locate any of them.

"There you are!" a loud voice shouted. I turned to see Franchesca Simmbaba pushing her way through the crowd to get to us. "Oh, you have been transformed into the creation of the year!" she exclaimed. "You both could not look any more beautiful, even if you tried!"

At that statement, I knew she had serious vision problems, but I just smiled. How could one reply to that statement, anyway?

"You have seen our friend, Nadir?" Lena asked her hopefully.

"My little precious one, I would not know if I had nor had not," Franchesca Simmbaba said with a grin. "I do not know what you are saying, nor do I care to know what is your intent." She stood there for a moment, looking at Lena and me, up and down, until she heaved a sigh of satisfaction. "Our artists have done wonders with you girls. You both look so angelic! I would not have even recognized you if I had not already known who you are."

I considered her statement for a few seconds and decided she did not require an answer, so I just nodded and smiled in agreement.

"What we are doing?" Lena asked Franchesca Simmbaba, a reasonable question.

"Oh, my little elfin one, I have no idea where you have been hiding," Franchesca Simmbaba said, with a chuckle in her voice. "Do you not pay attention to the activities of our community? Are you not well-versed in the events of the palace? Have you been holed-up in your compartment, not speaking and learning what is important around here?"

"I do not know," Lena answered honestly.

"Well, my fragile little waif," Franchesca Simmbaba said, as she leaned down so her eyes would be on the same level as Lena's, "you do ask an important question. So many people take for granted the procedure and they do not follow the royal guidelines.

"Now we are in the procession to be introduced to the royal family. First, each of us will go to the table of preparation, where we are to dip our fingers three times in the royal bowl, which holds the water of cleansing. After the third dip, we are to wipe the remaining water of cleansing onto our hair. For those who are lacking a head full of hair, they have been provided with substitute gold or silver head coverings, to be used for the wiping of the cleansed fingertips."

I was beginning to understand that this community had too much idle time in their schedules, so much so that they needed to create senseless rituals to fill their days. Recalling the man's remark at the wedding ceremony, I understood that they had no religion here, no spiritual food for their souls, and I had seen no books or technology. From what I had observed, they had only three children in their entire society, so they had no need for formal education: no schools, no teachers, no classes, no ongoing learning. This community and their meaningless customs must be the result of an entire generation of people who felt they had reached the ultimate goal: to live without thinking and exist without growing. Someone must have done quite a lot of work in order for everything to arrive at this current state, but now that they were here, they had nothing important to do. Where were the cooks, the farmers, the planners and the organizers? Perhaps all the workers were somewhere behind the scenes, working?

"After our fingertips have been ceremoniously cleansed and dried, we will be permitted to enter the line for the greeting of the princes," Franchesca Simmbaba continued. "This is where you will need to watch what you say. If incorrect words are heard coming out of your mouth, you will be moved out of the line and not permitted to enter the line for the greeting of the Queen. You will still be allowed to go to the table of feasting and fill a plate with food, but you will be in the category of the disgraced, and will subsequently unable to join in the grand ball. You will be forced to the sidelines where you may merely watch and long to join in the festivities, but, as everyone knows, the disgraced may not participate.

"However, I know you two will not be disgraced by unlikely words coming out of your mouths, so you will be allowed to follow the procession of the royal path. When it is your turn, you will tell the royal assistant the name by which you choose to be called. The royal assistant, in turn, will tell the whisperer to the princes what that name is, and the princes, first Prince Arumbo and then Prince Botolo, will speak your name. You may then take a bow or curtsy, whichever is your preference, although I would recommend a curtsy, since those gowns do not appear to be optimized for taking a bow."

"I ask for your pardon," Lena said, as a look of worry crossed her face. "I do not know what is this 'curtsy' you are speaking. How am I to do it?"

"What?" Franchesca Simmbaba exclaimed, as if she couldn't believe her ears. "Have you not yet been trained in the royal matters?"

Lena shook her head slowly.

"It's like this," I said, speaking like an expert. I had seen it on old movies, but at the Complex, no one would ever have a reason to curtsy, so I had not actually done it before.

I put one foot behind the other and began to bend my knees, but with my giant golden bell-dress, I was unable to lower myself because the fabric was so stiff. The collar was so tight, I just about strangled myself. Lena laughed, and I realized she couldn't even see what I was doing with my legs, as they were hidden under the waist of the bell.

"This is what the princes want to see?" she giggled.

"Oh, my dear," Franchesca Simmbaba cried. "This will never do. In that dress, you cannot take a bow, and with your level of clumsiness, you are unable to curtsy. Perhaps you will be best off to take yourself out of the line of procession and head directly over to the table of feasting." She turned to Lena and put her hands on Lena's shoulders, smiling. "Our little elfin one may still be able to be introduced to the royals, but you, my dear," she waved her head in my direction, "will never be accepted without being able to be graceful."

This horrid dress was really causing me a ton of grief, and I wished I could simply jump out of it right now: but I could not. I tried to not let Franchesca Simmbaba's descriptions of my lack of gracefulness hurt my feelings. I needed to focus on my reason for being here, but, of necessity, that included meeting the princes so I could have a chance to get close to my mother.

"I do not go where Layla do not go," Lena announced. "We stay together."

"You little spunk!" Franchesca Simmbaba said playfully. "She will be right over there, with the other rejects. You do not want to willfully put your own self in that position, when you have such a matchless opportunity to be introduced to the royals. Come, come now, let us move along." She tried to guide Lena and keep her going with the line toward the treasured royals while at the same time snubbing me.

"No!" Lena insisted. "I go with Layla, or Layla come with me."

"I will go with you, Lena," I said, against the recommendation of Franchesca Simmbaba, who looked at me in unbelief.

"You shall not!" she said, stopping in her tracks, in an effort to block me from going in that direction.

"You do not speak to Layla in this manner," a powerful male voice said from behind us.

Lena and I both turned to see an extremely handsome man dressed in a shimmering silver suit towering over us.

"Nadir!" Lena exclaimed, leaping into his arms.

"Now, you are not exhibiting gracefulness, my little elfin one," Franchesca Simmbaba warned.

"You, old woman, stand off," Nadir said to Franchesca Simmbaba, as he wrapped his arms around Lena protectively.

His statement closed her mouth, and I saw the hurt in her eyes. I did not really feel sorry for her, though, because she was merely getting a taste of her own medicine. After all, she had just said very hurtful words to me; but still, to call a lady an 'old woman' might have been the worst insult possible.

Franchesca Simmbaba turned her back on us as our line moved forward and she prepared to be introduced to the princes.

"Where have you been?" I asked Nadir. "We were looking for you."

He set Lena on the ground and looked directly at her as he answered my question. "I was with you all the time," he said. "I did not let you out of my range of sight."

"But we were looking for you and we didn't see you," I said.

"I did follow you to the hair artist and I did wait for you until they finish with styling the hair of you and Lena," Nadir said. "Layla, you now have hair of a very unusual way."

"Thank you for putting it so kindly," I said with a smile. He could have said what he honestly thought, like he did with Franchesca Simmbaba, but instead, he made me feel like I did not have the funniest hairstyle in the entire world.

"The color of your hair is exactly the color of your dress," he stated.

"Yes, thank you for noticing," I said.

"Excuse me, Miss," a man in a uniform was saying loudly to Franchesca Simmbaba. "You must leave the procession to the royals at this time. You have been disgraced. You may eat from the table of feasting, but you may not join in the festivities nor may you interact with the accepted ones."

"What did I say?" Franchesca Simmbaba asked loudly. "What did I say?"

Two men in uniforms joined the one who had spoken to her and the three men escorted Franchesca Simmbaba from the line.

All of a sudden, Lena, Nadir and I were standing at the front of the line. I was unprepared as I stared at the four thrones before us, and the four people who were sitting in them. My eyes skirted over the two princes, looking much more relaxed than they had during the wedding ceremony, to rest upon the two brides. There they were, my mom and my Aunt Moon, sitting right in front of us, just a few steps away.

CHAPTER 14

"Your name?" asked a man who had come out of nowhere to stand beside me.

As I opened my mouth to answer, I was staring right into the eyes of my mother. She seemed to be very bored, looking right at me, but also right through me, just another subject of her royal kingdom. Yes, she was my mother, but she was changed. The spark was gone out of her eye, and I was unexpectedly reminded of my own self, my own life when I had been merely existing at the Complex, not living, without family and without love.

Skipping over the required curtsy, I inhaled deeply so that I could speak my name loudly enough for my mother to hear as I continued to look directly into her eyes.

At the exact instant I shouted, "Layla!" the sound of a mallet hitting the enormous brass disk resonated throughout the room, booming and echoing, completely covering the sound of my voice, and loud trumpets began to sound.

A ruckus off to my left, somewhere near where the Queen was sitting, drew the attention of everyone in the room, but I kept my eyes fixed on my mom, even as the wave of people began to wash in the direction of the Queen. My mom casually turned her head toward the Queen, and I reluctantly took my gaze off of my mom for just one second, which was long enough for me to know that nothing happening in the room was as important as my mom, and as I looked back at her, I saw the four thrones were being swallowed up by the walls.

My mom had been right here, and now she had

disappeared? In the chaos, I ran over to where her throne had been, searching for a way to open up the secret compartment that had engulfed my mom.

"Mom! Mom! Come back!" I shouted at the top of my lungs, unheard over the ruckus in the room. I couldn't believe my long-lost mother had disappeared right in front of me for the second time today.

"Come on!" a young voice yelled.

Before I knew what was happening, I was being tugged by two little hands in the opposite direction of where everyone else was going. As I tried to get my bearings, I realized that my two little brothers were both pulling me out of the confusion to the other side of the room. We arrived at a stairway where they led me up several flights of stairs. I struggled to go up, up, up, from one landing to the next, in this dress that was not exactly flexible. I could tell it had been made for a lady to dance, not to climb stairs. I finally made it to the top of the flights of stairs. Following the boys, I stepped into a long hallway which I recognized to be the same hallway we had been in earlier today, when Uncle Pierce and I were first brought into the palace by one of the twins. The boys began to run down the hall, but I was out of breath and could not take another step.

"Wait!" I said, huffing and puffing.

They stopped running and turned around to watch me as I struggled to make my way to them.

"You look like a giant bell," one said, "and now it looks like you are ringing, moving back and forth like that."

"Be quiet!" the other boy said. "That is not a nice thing to say."

"Mother always tells us to be honest and speak the truth." The way he said 'Mother' kind of tugged on my heart, but I kept walking.

"But we are not to say things that are not nice."

"Bells are nice! They are really pretty!"

I finally caught up with them. I decided to disregard their conversation and get down to business.

"So, you know who I am?" I asked.

"Of course! You are Layla. We know all about you."

"Yeah, but we didn't know you got so old already."

I was beginning to despise this community's obsession with making sure people knew they were old.

"And you are my brothers?" I said, not intending it to come out as a question, but it did.

"If you are our sister, we have to be your brothers, don't you know anything?"

"I don't know your names," I said.

"What kind of a sister are you, anyway?"

"I am your sister who didn't even know about you until today!"

My brothers looked at each other. Apparently they had not been aware of this fact until now.

"You were born after The Great Devastation," I explained.

"The what?"

"I mean, I haven't seen our mother since before you were born!"

"Why not?" Two blended voices asked. Two identical faces were looking at me with the same question mark on them. "Where have you been all this time anyway?"

"I was living in another place, a place we called the Complex."

"No, there's no other place to live," one brother insisted. "Everybody in the world lives here."

"You have a lot to learn." I told him. "There are lots of places where people live besides here."

"Like where?" the other brother asked. "Some complex place? Whatever that means."

"Well, there's the Complex, where I came from," I explained patiently, "and lots of people live there, and then there's Mountain Veil, way on the other side of the world, and a bunch of people live there, and then there are a whole bunch other places like small towns, all over the place, where people live."

"You are lying!" one boy said.

"It's not nice to call a person a liar," the other boy said.

"There's no other places where people live!" the first boy shouted.

The boys started to wrestle and argue and sort of punch each other.

"Stop!" I said, trying to calm them. "So, how did you recognize me at that party? I don't even look at all like myself."

"I've been watching you all day," one brother said.

"But I haven't seen you since the wedding."

"I can see everything from my room upstairs," he said.

"Oh, okay, so… tell me, what are your names?" I asked.

"I am Danny, and this is David," one of them said.

"No, I am Daniel, and he is David," the other one said.

One started pushing the other and they had a miniature fight right in front of me.

"Stop it! Stop it!" I said.

"Okay, I am David and he is Danny," the first one said.

"He just said he is Danny because David always gets in trouble," Daniel said.

"You didn't have to tell her that," David said.

"Okay, you are David, and you are Daniel," I said, trying to see how I was going to tell them apart. "So, take me to our mom!"

"We can't go to her now," David said.

"Why not?" I asked.

"Because they're locked in the chambers," Daniel said.

"And nobody can go in the chambers unless the princes let them in," David said.

"Well, they will let me in, because she is my mom and I haven't seen her in all these years," I said, coming to the logical conclusion.

"Wow! How did you do that?" David asked, giving me a funny look.

"How did I do what?" I asked.

"Your hair!" Daniel exclaimed. "It's all lighting up!"

"Yeah, it's like it has little sparkly things all over it, little lights on your head, glowing in the dark."

"How can I get this ridiculous thing off my head?" I asked, moving my hands around it, but afraid to touch it.

"You're going to have to go back to the artistic stylist," David said.

"Yeah, but you can't do that now," Daniel said, "because everybody is downstairs right now."

"You mean, everybody except our mom," I clarified.

"Well, yeah, our mom, our aunt, and the princes and the Queen," Daniel said.

"Well, what if it's a hair emergency?" I asked.

Both boys laughed.

"A hair emergency!" they said at the same time. "What does that mean?"

"Well, just look at my hair," I said. "This is an emergency and I went to get it undone right now, especially if I can't see Mom right now. I really don't want to meet her looking like this. Maybe we can take these lights out."

"I wouldn't try it," Daniel warned.

"You wouldn't try anything," David said, "because you are too scared."

I stepped between them before they could launch into another altercation.

"So, they are going to continue the celebration, even though everyone was going wild down there?" I asked. "I thought the whole point of it was so everybody could meet the royal people."

"No, the whole point of it is to have a big party, like they do all the time," Daniel said rolling his eyes.

"Everybody already knows the Queen and the princes."

"That means there is no way to get in to see our mom?" I asked. "When will we be able to see her again?"

"Probably tomorrow, or the next day," David said.

"So, you are saying there is no way we can see her tonight?" This was more than a little frustrating to me.

"Right, there's no way," Daniel said.

"So, then, where do you go when you can't be with your mom?" I asked.

"We will just go back to our rooms upstairs," Daniel said.

"Wait, you live upstairs in the castle?" I asked.

"It's not a castle, it's a palace. Don't you know anything?" David said, rolling his eyes.

"Be nice to her, David!" Daniel said. "She's our sister, and she's really nice."

I suddenly had a great idea - and these were the boys to get the job done.

"Where would they take somebody who was captured?" I asked.

"Nobody ever gets captured around here. What are you talking about?"

"Remember during the wedding, those two men who were taken away because they were interrupting the wedding? Where were they taken?"

My brothers looked at each other. They looked at me. They didn't say anything.

"What? What? Why are you looking like that?" I asked.

"Who cares where they are?" David shrugged. "We

don't know who those guys are."

Daniel shook his head and also shrugged.

"I know who they are," I said mysteriously.

That got their attention.

"Who? Who are they?" Daniel asked.

"Tell me where they are, and I will tell you who they are," I promised.

"We told you, we don't know where they are," Daniel said.

"I know where they might be," David said, raising one eyebrow.

"How do you know?" Daniel said. "You don't know everything."

"I am pretty sure I know where they are," David said, nodding.

"Do you think they are downstairs at the celebration?" I asked.

"No, they wouldn't let them come to the celebration, because they are troublemakers," Daniel said.

"So, where would troublemakers be?" I asked.

"We don't know where they take troublemakers," Daniel said. "They are just gone for a while and then they come back here and they are not troublemakers anymore."

"I know where they are," David said, giving us a rebellious look. "But why should I tell you? How do I know you are not going to get me in trouble?"

"Because," I said, lowering my voice and bending down to be at eye level with them, the best as I could in the bell of a dress, even though there was no one else anywhere near us, "one of those troublemakers is our dad."

CHAPTER 15

"I knew it!" David shouted. "That was our dad with you when I saw you earlier, right? But I asked him and he said he is not my dad."

"You saw them earlier?" Daniel asked, with a look of shock on his face. "Before the wedding? You saw our dad and you didn't tell me?"

"No, that was our Uncle Pierce with me when you brought us into the palace," I explained, this time making sure I didn't refer to it as a castle.

"You brought them into the palace?" Daniel asked. He lunged into David and they started fighting with each other again.

"We only came through here, and then we went out by going down the secret slide," I said, trying to ease things over between them.

"You took them all the way upstairs, to the prince's chambers, and let them go down the emergency exit ramp?" Daniel doubled his efforts to subdue his twin.

"No, I didn't take them up there!" David said, holding off Daniel's wild punches. "They were already up there!"

"How could they get all the way upstairs, past the guards and everyone?" Daniel asked.

"They just did!" David said. "I don't know how they got up there! They were just there, so I helped them get out!"

"It's impossible for anyone to get up there!" Daniel said, as he got our brother into a hold, locking his hands behind him. "You took them up there, and you are really going to get in trouble for doing it! I am going to tell Mom!"

"No, David, I mean, Daniel, he is right," I said. "Stop fighting! We were already up there, and he showed us the way down and out."

Daniel stopped squeezing and looked at me suspiciously.

"We were lost, walking around up in the desert, and we saw this golden glowing thing and we felt the buzzing, so we walked toward it. Then David came and showed us how to get down into the canyon," I explained, trying to get David out of trouble.

"You went outside?" Daniel asked, suddenly releasing David, and giving him a little shove. "You are really going to get in trouble! You know we are not to go up there, ever!"

David stepped back, not returning the aggression. "I go up there all the time, and I never get in trouble. And if you don't tell, no one will ever know!"

Daniel looked at him with unbelief.

"You better not tell, I am warning you," David said, making a fist.

"Yeah? Who is going to stop me?" Daniel asked.

I could see they were about to get into it again, so I stepped between them.

"You guys! We have to go find our dad, and I mean, now!" I said, redirecting them to our current urgent goal. "Where do you think he is?"

David looked around me to look at Daniel, then he looked up at me.

"Where is he?" I asked again.

"We will have to go outside," he said. "YOU don't have to go with us. You can stay here, if you are afraid to get in trouble."

"And let you find our dad without me?" Daniel said, as he tried to act brave. I could sense the apprehension in his voice, and I could relate to him. After all, I had lived nearly nine years in the Complex, and I did have a fear all that time of breaking the rules. Now I knew that some rules, such as the ones that were made just to control people and didn't have any other purpose, could be broken and the entire society would not fall to pieces.

"We all have to go," I suggested. "He has to see all of us together. But if we are going outside, I have to take off this ridiculous dress."

A picture popped up in my mind: my backpack with my regular clothes in it, back at the place where I had been dressed in my big golden bell outfit.

"Yeah, you will be attracting all the snakes and vultures and stuff, with those lights on your head and feet," David snickered.

"Maybe we need the lights, because it is getting dark outside," Daniel said. At first, I thought he must be kidding, but he was serious.

"One problem: my clothes are back at the clothing shop," I said.

"Clothing shop?" Daniel asked, shaking his head. "What is a clothing shop?"

"The place where I was forced into this ugly thing!" I shouted, not intending to be frustrated, but at this point, I couldn't help it. I was really uncomfortable.

"Oh, you are talking about the artistic fashion

center," David said, with a touch of pride in his voice.

"Well, whatever they call it, that is where my clothes are now," I said. "I need to get them, because those are clothes I can wear outside and move around quickly." This statement was a bit of a stretch, because by now every one of my muscles was aching from all the new kinds of activity they had experienced over the last few days, but I would be able to move more quickly in clothes were made to be lived in, than in this thing that was nothing more than a decoration floating about my body.

"We can get you some other clothes," Daniel said tentatively. "I am sure we can find something for you to wear. I can ask one of the servants."

"No!" David said. "We can't tell anyone! Then they will know we are going outside! We have to change our clothes, too. Are you dumb or something? Do you think we can just go across the desert in these things?"

"Don't call me dumb!" Daniel said. "Everyone knows I am smarter than you are!"

I was expecting David to lunge at Daniel and start another fight, but instead, he just gave a slight smile, keeping his cool.

"If you are so smart," David said quietly, "why do I know more than you do about this matter?"

"What matter are you talking about?" Daniel said, putting his fists up in front of his chests.

"I know where our dad is, and you don't." David stood his ground.

Daniel dropped his fists. "That is just because you are always going where you shouldn't be going, and snooping into everyone else's business instead of doing what you should be doing!"

"Come on, stop fighting!" I urged.

"We are not fighting!" David said.

"Well, we better get going if we are going to find Dad, and you said you can find some more appropriate clothes for me to wear," I reminded them.

"Follow me, I know where all the best clothes are." David took off running down the hallway, so we hurried after him. He stopped at one doorway and waited for us to catch up to him.

"We can't go in there!" Daniel cried.

"I go in here all the time," David said, and by his actions and attitude, I believed him.

We stepped into a giant room that was filled with racks of clothes of all colors, styles and sizes. At first the lighting was very dim. As we began to move about in the room, it began to glow slowly, and was soon fully lit.

"What is this place?" I asked, as I began to search for a suitable outfit.

"This is one of the royal clothing rooms," David said. He had made a beeline to one side of the room where he must have known were clothing of his size. Daniel walked slowly behind him, taking in the sights of the room.

"I think this will fit me," I said, pulling a plain outfit from one of the racks.

"Those are boy clothes," Daniel said, looking back at me. He was stopping and feeling the fabrics, which, I was surprised to discover, were each so pleasing to the touch.

"I don't care," I said, stepping behind a large rack of

clothing for a bit of privacy. "This is what I am going to wear, because it is the most sensible."

Both boys began to laugh.

"What?" I asked. "What is so funny?" I was already out of the golden bell dress, just slightly regretting that I had heard it tear while I was removing it. I had to peel the glowing tubes off my feet, and, oh, what a relief to have my toes free from that bindery!

"This whole place exists because no one is the most sensible," one of the twins said.

"That is what Mom always says," the other twin added. I could hear them rustling in the clothing on the other side of the room.

"Okay, now, where are the shoes?" I asked, stepping out from my semi-private place.

"Two rooms down," one of the twins, presumably David, answered. "Let's all go and find something, what did you call it? Appropriate? I like that word."

The boys had selected very sensible outfits that were not that different from mine: pants and top in shades of dull green with light brown trim.

"I guess if you have to dress like a boy, it is good that you are dressed like us," one twin said.

"Just a minute," I said. "Now that you have changed, you have to let me know, which one is Daniel and which one is David?"

They exchanged glances.

"Come on! I am your sister! Let's get serious, so we can go and find our dad!"

The one on my left admitted, "I am David." The other one nodded, so I was satisfied. His statement was confirmed when the one who said he was David led us to the shoe room.

Again, the lighting was dim and began to glow as we entered. In this room must have been all the shoes that had ever existed in the Time Before. Shelves and shelves that were tilted at a slight angle displayed shoes of every size, every color, and every style, from the most fancy shoes that looked like they were covered in diamonds, to the most rugged climbing boots. The shoes were arranged in order of the colors of the rainbow: yellow to orange to red to purple to blue to green, with a variety of shades in between them. The room itself was so beautiful, an artistic creation merely in the placement of the shoes. I had never been much interested in shoes, especially coming from a society where the look of one's footwear had absolutely no importance, but now I was transfixed. I could not stop staring at all these shoes, thousands of pairs, and they all seemed to be calling out to me, "I would look beautiful on your feet!"

"Come on, Layla," David said, pulling my arm. "Snap out of it! We have to get our shoes on and get going!"

His voice pulled me out of my daydream and we went over to the area where the useful shoes were: the boots, the rugged shoes, the ones that were not mere designs for the feet. They were also very nice shoes, but they were what they were: useful.

"These all look like they are brand new," I said, noting that not one shoe had a scratch or blemish on it, not even a bit of dirt.

"These shoes have never been worn," David said, pulling a pair of short boots off the shelf. "I need to see if these will fit me."

"What?" Daniel asked angrily. "You brought us to the shoe museum? We can't wear these shoes! They are for display only! I can't believe you would bring us here! We haven't even been allowed in this area yet!"

"We have to find our dad, remember?" David said, as he pushed his foot into the boot. "Oh, yeah, that feels good."

Daniel reluctantly took a very similar pair from the shelf and put them on. I had a harder time finding a good pair that fit me. The first two pairs I tried on squeezed and crushed my already sore feet. Finally, the third pair felt good on my feet, with a nice cushion and padding inside the rugged exterior that, surprisingly, looked very fashionable; that is to say, to a person who might have been interested in shoe fashions.

"Do we need a jacket?" I asked, after we hid our old shoes in a compartment that David knew about and were out in the hallway again. I was imagining another huge room filled with a nice variety of jackets and coats to keep us warm on this journey.

"It never gets cold here," Daniel said. "We don't wear jackets."

"Not even at night?" I asked. I kind of liked this idea of being in warm weather, day and night.

"Like he said, it NEVER gets cold here," David said. "Come on, this way."

"We are not allowed to go down there," Daniel warned.

"Yeah, and we are not allowed to be up here, either," David reminded him.

"Hey!" a voice shouted from a long ways down the hall. "What are you doing up here? Who is that?

Identify yourselves, immediately!"

"Come on!" David said, pulling my arm down the hall, away from the man's voice. "Hurry up!"

"Stop!" the man yelled. "I command you to stop!"

CHAPTER 16

We were already well on our way, and we were not about to stop and interfere with our mission to go and find our dad. In a couple of minutes we were once again inside the cave-stairway where David had brought Uncle Pierce and me, either a hundred years ago, or earlier this morning. We climbed up the stone steps, went back through the hidden door, and soon we were up on top, standing in the desert.

"Will he follow us up here?" I asked, once again trying to catch my breath.

"No, he doesn't even know about the upper passageway," David said with certainty.

"Well, maybe we better hurry along and get away from here," I suggested.

We ran for a couple of minutes in the opposite direction from where Uncle Pierce and I had come, but then I had to stop and walk. My brothers slowed to a walk with me.

"You come up here all the time?" Daniel asked. "When? When do you have time to come up here?"

"When you are studying," David asked. "You can't learn anything listening to those crazy people. They don't even notice when I leave the room."

"Yes, they do notice when you leave," Daniel said. "They are just afraid to tell anyone."

"Yeah, we can get away with just about anything," David said.

"And why is that?" I asked. I was already getting to know my brothers. Daniel was very safe and obedient while David was adventurous and rebellious. In our current situation, both types of personalities would come in handy.

"Because we are the only kids," David said, confirming my earlier suspicions. "We and Jasper are the only kids here in our community."

"Yeah, after The Great Devastation, well, not too long before you were born, when we had the big war and everything, something happened that made it really hard for babies to be born," I said, thinking about how the ones at the Complex had done everything they could to try to find any women who were not sterile.

"You mean, we are the only kids in the whole world?" Daniel asked. "I thought you said there are a lot of other communities all over the world."

"No, I am just saying there are not really very many kids, especially ones as young as you are, or younger than you. And there are not a lot of other communities, but there are some. I was just saying that this is not the only community in the world."

"Are we just going to talk the whole way, and walk this slow?" David asked. "Because if we do, it is going to take forever to get to where our dad is."

"Well come on, let's step on it!" I said. They gave me a strange look. "Let's hurry!" I clarified, and we began to walk quickly across the desert. The sun was just setting, so it was no longer hot out there. The temperature was actually quite pleasant.

"If we want to get there before dark, we will have to take the short cut," David said.

"Short cuts are good!" I said, already breathing hard.

"This way might be a little bit scary," David warned.

"What do you mean by that?" Daniel asked.

"Well, it is much shorter, so we will save a lot of time, like a few hours, but we have to go down a different way."

"Have you gone this way before?" I asked. "Have you taken the short cut?"

"Yeah, a few times," David said with confidence. "I was the one who made it like this."

"Made it like what?" I asked.

"You will see, if you want to go that way," David said. "We have to decide now, because here is where the paths split up. This one, on the right, goes to the short cut, and the one on the left goes around the long way. It goes down by where we were for the wedding ceremony, well, it splits into two, and the other way it goes all the way around, to where they take the troublemakers."

I looked down both paths. They both went off into the distance, and neither one looked any more perilous than the other. The longer way did appear to have a slight downward slope, while the short cut had a bit of an incline.

"Which one has more snakes?" I asked, thinking about my lighted head and how the boys had mentioned it would attract those scary creatures.

"Well, they both probably have the same amount of snakes, but this way they would be more spread out because we would walk a much farther distance.

I began to feel very skittish, looking to my left and right for possible snakes.

"Let's take the short cut," I said, just wanting to get to my dad as soon as we possibly could. I was too tired to walk for several more hours, but I didn't want to tell my little brothers that.

We took the path to the right and began to walk quickly.

"You know, actually the lights on your head might scare the snakes away," Daniel said. "We learned that snakes like the dark. That is why they hide under rocks."

After hearing this fact, which I chose to believe, I began to walk with my head held high, even putting it out in front of me, in an effort to keep all snakes out of our path.

"At least we won't lose sight of you," David said. "Your head is really glowing now."

Daniel gave a slight snicker but didn't say anything.

After a few minutes of walking in silence, David spoke up. "We better run for a little bit, so we can get to the cliffs before dark. I don't see the moon coming up yet, and we will want to be able see."

"Cliffs?" I asked. "You didn't say anything about cliffs when we were back there, choosing which way to go."

"I said it was more scary," David said.

"We are not going to have to climb up a cliff, are we?" I asked. My leg muscles could not do that at this time.

"No, of course we don't have to climb up a cliff," David said. "We get to go down one."

"Um, my brother, that sounds pretty dangerous," Daniel said, with a great deal of hesitancy in his voice.

"You are afraid of everything," David said. "Why don't you just go back and sit in your room and wait for tomorrow or the next day, when they give you permission to come out again?"

"Oh, no! No you don't! I am going to meet our dad at the same time as you," Daniel said.

"It's not that bad," David reassured us. "We will put on the harnesses and just go right down, nice and easy."

"Go right down a cliff, nice and easy?" I asked. "Nice and easy down a cliff?"

"I said it might be a little scary," David said, "I did not say it would be dangerous. That was Danny's voice speaking fear, not mine."

"I am not afraid!" Daniel insisted.

"Come on, guys, stop arguing!" I pleaded. "Let us just get to this cliff and go down it, nice and easy." I was aware that I was trying to convince myself with my brave words.

"Okay, there it is," David said.

Up ahead of us, I could see the silhouette of a cluster of trees.

"I see trees," I said, relieved to be near our destination.

"Be careful when you get near the trees," David said. "The cliff edge is right there."

Daniel and I slowed our pace while David led the way. My heart was doing that thing where it felt like it was fluttering and stopping. As we stepped between the last trees in the cluster, I grabbed onto one of the branches to keep my balance. I did not like heights. Although I had been in very few high places in my life, even watching a movie with great heights made my feet feel all tingly on the bottom. I carefully looked over the edge of the cliff. At this very moment, my feet were tingling so much that I was afraid they were both going to fall asleep.

Down below us was a large area partially enclosed by a circular canyon. I could just make out in the distance where the path coming around from the long way entered, straight ahead of us. Yes, this certainly was a short cut, but the distance difference was made up in height. We were at the top of a very high cliff, just steps away from a sheer drop, a drop that must go straight down. I was not quite ready to get to the edge of the cliff, so I stood there, tightly gripping the branch of the tree.

"What is that white stuff?" Daniel asked, as he approached the ledge.

"What white stuff?" I asked. I didn't even want to look at his close proximity to the edge.

"Oh, that's just ice," David said nonchalantly.

"Ice?" I said, trying my best to not let a sound of alarm creep into my voice.

"Yeah, it will help us slide down easier," David said.

"I am not going to slide down a cliff on ice," I said. "I think we should go back, and go the other way."

"No, we can't!" David insisted. "I think I see them down there!"

He was standing right at the edge, looking down. Daniel eased up to stand beside him.

"That is our dad down there?" Daniel asked excitedly.

"I can't quite see him from here," I said, still gripping the tree branch.

"It's too far away to see his face," David said, "but

I know that is him. This is where they bring all the troublemakers, and they stay here until they can behave and come back to the community. If they don't want to behave, they can leave, and they go off that other way, and they never come back."

"How do you know all this?" Daniel asked. "I never heard of them taking away a troublemaker and then letting him come back."

"You don't know anything," David said. "All you do is listen to whatever they want you to know. From up here, I can hear what they say down there."

"What are they saying now?" I asked, straining to hear my dad's voice.

"They are not talking now," David said, "I think they are eating. They have a little fire and they are sitting by it. Four people are by the fire and they must have two guards standing way over there."

My stomach growled, and I tried to remember the last time I had eaten. I suddenly felt weak, unable to go any further.

"We need to go down now," David said.

"I don't think I should go right now," I said, trying to think up a good excuse.

"Here, Layla, come over here, and I will put this harness on you. Then I can lower you down."

"You are going to lower me down? I don't think you can hold my weight."

"No, Silly, the harness is connected to the tree, that big, fat one, right there. It has two ropes, one for up and one for down, so I pull this one up, and you go down with the other one."

"I don't think so," I said, looking in the other direction. "How far back was that other path?"

"Our dad is right there!" David said. "You have to tell him who we are. We have never met him before. Come on, don't be scared."

"What about the ice?" I asked.

"Oh, it will be behind you," David said. "You will be facing out that way, and the ice will be at your back, so you will just slide down it."

A shiver ran through me as I thought about sliding down a cliff on a huge slice of ice.

"I'll go first," Daniel offered.

"No, Layla should go first," David said. "Come on, our dad is RIGHT THERE. We need to get down there."

I slowly released my hold on the tree branch and took a couple of steps toward my brothers. David was holding some sort of contraption that had ropes and straps. The tingling in my feet was turned up to the highest setting and I began to feel a little bit dizzy.

"I don't know--" I started to say, but David was already busy wrapping me in straps and tugging on ropes.

"Okay, you are ready," he said, although I was not.

"Are you sure this is safe?" I asked, wanting nothing more than to get out of it. I would force myself to run the entire long way, if I could only be released from this thing and this experience.

"Just step right over here, and I will let you down, nice and easy, a little bit at a time."

My little brother, whom I had just met today, was asking me to step off a cliff and slide down a giant chunk of ice. I took a small step, trying to see the fire and the ones sitting around it.

"Come on, you are almost there," David urged.

I took another tentative step, pulling together everything inside of me to get enough courage, when suddenly, I was pushed over the edge and my feet were hanging useless beneath me. I lost my breath and my back began to freeze at the same instant as I was dangling over the edge of a cliff by something an eight-year-old was calling a harness. As I moved slowly, slowly downward, tightly gripping the straps that were across my chest, I was at first still afraid to look down. As a matter of fact, for a few moments, I kept my eyes pressed tightly closed. I did not want to see myself as I went crashing to the ground. My mind automatically began a prayer, asking God to forgive me and thanking Him for at least letting me see my mother and dad again before I died, and then, thanking him for the twin brothers I didn't know I had until today. Their voices, coming from way up above me, would be the last voices I would ever hear.

As I began to focus on their voices, I realized that I was not dying – not yet – and I heard the twins arguing again as I was sliding down the ice, bit by bit. Their voices grew faint, and I heard another voice – my dad's voice! I opened my eyes to discover that I was indeed approaching the ground, but because of the formation of rock sticking out beside me, I was unable to see anyone from where I was.

I noticed that my back was no longer against the ice, but I was just hanging out there. I looked up above me, but by now it was too dark to see anything in that direction. I was only able to see the ground because of the light that was coming from the fire.

After the longest few minutes of my life, my feet were finally on solid ground. I regretted at this moment that I had not been paying attention when David had strapped this harness thing on me, because I could not figure out how to get it off. I was fiddling with it, trying to make it go this way or that, or to at least loosen up a bit so I would be able to wiggle out of it.

"Hi, Sister!" a little voice beside me said, surprising me. A close look let me know that Daniel had made it down the icy cliff and he quickly removed his harness. "Do you want me to help you with that?" he asked, coming over to me, touching a couple of spots, and watching as the harness dropped from me. "Good thing your hair glows in the dark, so Davy didn't let me down right on top of you."

"Yes, that is a good thing," I said, wondering how many more jokes I would need to hear about my hair, but at the same time, grateful that it was at least useful.

"Here comes Davy," Daniel said, looking up, over my head.

I instinctively stepped away from the rock wall to give David room to land and tried to see him in the darkness.

"Ahhh!" he yelled, from a short distance above us.

At that moment everything seemed to happen at once: the sound of ice crackling, voices shouting, Daniel pushing me to one side, and David landing on me, knocking me to the ground.

"Ow, ow!" David said, with a strained voice. He and I began to untangle our limbs and his ropes as I tried to decide what part of me hurt the most.

"I am so sorry," Daniel was saying, "I was trying to push you out of the way, but then he was falling sideways!"

"What on earth is this glowing helmet?" a voice asked, adding an insult to my injuries.

"Where did you kids come from?"

"What are you doing here?"

"He fell!" Daniel shouted.

Immediately we were surrounded by people.

"Are you all right?"

"How far did you fall?"

"What do you have on your head? Where did you get a helmet that glows in the dark?"

"Dad!" I was able to say.

"Layla, is that you?" my dad asked, instantly by my side. "What are you doing? How did you find me? What happened to your hair?"

"Layla, thank goodness!" Uncle Pierce said. "We were so worried about you. How did you get here?"

"Pierce, you really should be thanking God, not goodness," my dad said, forever the chaplain.

"Why would you thank Someone who does not exist?" a man asked. "We have all agreed that there is no God."

"Just agreeing upon a concept does not make it true," my dad said, as David and I were finally two separate people again. "If everyone agreed that the law of gravity was not a good law and you voted to repeal it, would it make it void?"

"What do you mean?" the man asked.

"These children just came down the side of this cliff with the help of the law of gravity. If everyone agreed that gravity did not exist, would they have just remained up there, floating in the air?" My dad was holding me, feeling for broken bones.

"No, of course not."

"It is the same way with God," my dad said. "You can believe in Him or not believe in Him, but nothing you do makes a difference in His existence. He is still God, whether you say so or not."

"That is one way of looking at it, I guess," the man said.

"That is the right way of looking at it," I said.

"Does anything hurt?" my dad asked me.

"No, just… everything," I said, feeling all these little aches and pains where David had landed on me.

"Do you think you can stand up?" my dad said, assisting me.

"Yeah, I am okay, too," David said. "Now, which one of you is our dad?"

CHAPTER 17

"What are you talking about?" all the men asked at the same time. We were still in the dark, with the only light coming from my glowing helmet-hair.

"Why do you keep asking me that question?" Uncle Pierce asked.

"Can we go sit by the fire?" I asked, wanting to get a bit more light on our little party.

"Let me help you," my dad said, taking my arm to steady me, as we went around the corner of the rock and headed over to the fire.

"Yeah, I am okay, I can make it by myself," David pouted. "I don't need help like my baby sister."

That stopped my dad in his tracks. "What did you say?" He turned to face David.

"Are you my dad?" David asked. He looked at Uncle Pierce. "Or, are you?"

"David, Daniel, this is our dad," I said. "Dad, meet my twin brothers. This is David and this is Daniel."

My dad nearly dropped me. We took the few steps to the fire and we sat on the blankets they had arranged as seats around it.

"What are you saying?" my dad asked.

"Mom was pregnant at the time of The Great Devastation," I explained, "with twins. And here they are."

In the light of the fire, I could see that my dad was crying.

"Hi, Dad," Daniel said, extending his hand for a handshake.

"Come here," my dad said, opening his arms. Both boys fell into them and the three of them hugged for a few minutes. My dad kept crying, without speaking, until the boys slowly pulled away from him to sit beside him. He kept his arms around them. "You both look just like Layla did when she was your age."

"Now her hair is really funny," Daniel said. "I hope mine doesn't get like that when I get old."

"This is not my real hair!" I said defensively. "And I am not OLD!"

"Layla," Uncle Pierce said, "aren't you forgetting something?"

"Yes, I am starving," I said. My stomach growled loudly to confirm it.

"No, I mean, your manners," Uncle Pierce said, nodding his head at me suggestively.

"Oh! I forgot! Uncle Pierce, these are my twin brothers, Daniel and David," I said, pointing to each one so Uncle Pierce could see which was which. "Daniel and David, this is our Uncle Pierce."

"How are you my uncle?" David asked, as he reached to shake Uncle Pierce's hand.

"My wife's sister is your mother," Uncle Pierce said.

"So you are Jasper's dad," Daniel stated.

"Who?" Uncle Pierce asked with a start.

"Our cousin, Jasper," Daniel said. "He was born two days after we were."

"I have a son?" Uncle Pierce asked. Now it was his turn to just about fall over. "Where is he?"

"He is back at the palace," David said. "He never gets in trouble, kind of like Daniel."

"What is he doing at the palace?" Uncle Pierce asked. "Come on, let's go! We have to go, now!" He was on his feet before I even knew what was happening.

"Wait a minute, Buddy," one of the other men said, leaping to his feet. Until now, they had just let us talk, but now he meant business. "You are not going anywhere. Troublemakers are to stay here for three days, until you decide if you want to abide by our rules and come back and live with us, or if you want to take the other path and go out to the desert and never come back. You are only on day one. You must stay here until we release you, in two days."

"But we have to get back right now!" I begged. "My mom and Aunt Moon are there, and if we don't get there in time, they are going to be married to the princes."

"What are you talking about?" the man asked. "Were you not a witness to the wedding? They are already married!"

"No, they can't be!" I shouted.

"Well, it is a good thing that you are here, away from the community, because you are acting like these troublemakers."

"No, I am NOT a troublemaker! I just want to go back to my mother!" I insisted.

"Did you see her?" my dad asked eagerly. "Did you talk to her? Did she recognize you?"

"I saw her when we went to the celebration at the palace, but she didn't recognize me because of this stupid glowing hair and my puffy red face." I recalled her bored expression as she sat upon the throne. "She didn't look like herself."

"Well, she is a little older," my dad said.

"No, it wasn't that," I said, trying to pinpoint the real problem. "Her eyes just looked so… dull or something. I don't think she even saw me. She was sitting there, on that throne, and she was just kind of staring. I don't think she actually saw anyone."

"Did you talk to her?" my dad asked. "What did you say? What did she say? You told her who you are, didn't you?"

"I was right at the front of the line, but at the exact second when I was saying my name, a loud noise sounded so she couldn't hear me. No one could hear me above the sound of the blast. I opened my mouth to speak, and all she could hear was 'waaaaaaa!' and then all kinds of chaos broke loose and Mom disappeared into the wall, her whole chair and everything."

"She disappeared into the wall?" my dad asked.

"Did you see Moon?" Uncle Pierce asked.

"Yes, Mom did disappear, and yes, I did see Aunt Moon," I said. "I don't know what happened, but the wall opened and Mom went into it, and so did Aunt Moon. Their chairs, along with the chairs where the princes were sitting, were sucked into the wall and then they were gone. Everyone in the whole room started going this way and that, and then Daniel and David started pulling me out of the room and we went upstairs--" I cut off my telling of the story at that point so those guard guys would not get my brothers in trouble.

"Someone pushed the panic button," Daniel said, glancing sideways at David. "We saw what was happening and we didn't want our sister, Layla, to be pushed and shoved in the crowds, so we took her out of there, the other way, with us, so she would be safe."

"Yeah, she doesn't know her way around the palace like we do," David added. "We just found her so we wanted to take care of her."

"Well, how about if we settle in for the night?" my dad said. "We can't go anywhere at night, and your Uncle Pierce and I need to stay here for a couple of days. In the morning, you can go back and let your mother and Aunt Moon know that we are here, and that after we learn our lesson, we will come back and meet you there."

"No!" I protested. "I am not going to leave you here. We need to stay together."

"I understand what you are saying, but we need to follow the rules," my dad said.

"Since we are not from here, we can't really do anything else," Uncle Pierce added.

"Aren't you tired?" my dad asked. "I know I am."

"Do you have anything to eat?" I asked timidly.

"We have a few crackers and some cheese left over," Uncle Pierce said. "How does that sound?"

"Perfect," I answered, taking a small packet from him. Before I took the first bite I asked, "Does anyone else want some?"

"No, we ate at the celebration," David said. "There was so much food on the feasting table, I am stuffed."

"You ate from the feasting table, before they said we could eat?" I asked.

David leaned over close to me. "I told you, we can do whatever we want," he said quietly. "We were hungry, so we ate."

"Let us bless the food," my dad said. This time, the

other man, the one who didn't believe in God, didn't say anything.

"Heavenly Father, we thank You so much, for what You have done, for what You are doing, and for what You are going to do. Bless this food as nourishment for our bodies, and make little become much. In the mighty name of Jesus we pray. Amen."

"Wow!" David said. "You always do that, don't you? Just like Mom said!"

"Yeah, she told us that you bless your food every time, right before you eat, right out loud so everyone can hear you."

"I am not ashamed to thank the Lord," my dad said.

"That is exactly what Mom said that you always say!" Daniel said enviously.

I felt just a tiny bit of jealousy because my two brothers had been with our mom all their lives, and I had been separated from her for nearly half of my life. My jealousy quickly passed when I considered that I had been with both of our parents for the first part of my life, and now, we were going to be all together, for the first time. I could just about imagine the look on my mom's face when she would see us, all of us – her three children and her husband – coming back into her life at the same time.

I quickly devoured the cheese and crackers. As soon as I was finished, I became extremely sleepy.

"Can I put my head on your lap for a minute, Daddy?"

"Come on over, my little La-la," he said, extending his arm. Before I knew what was happening, my two little brothers were snuggled up beside me. I fell asleep within a few seconds.

"Come on, let's go," a voice was whispering in my ear. I was in the middle of a dream, but those words snapped me wide awake in an instant. In a few seconds, my eyes had adjusted to the dark. My head felt a little funny, and a touch to my hair revealed that someone had wrapped a scarf or something around it, probably to hide my glowing hairstyle. A few aches and pains reminded me of the extra use I had been giving my muscles, as well as my brave act of catching my falling brother. After a bit of effort, I was able to get to my feet. I saw my dad and Uncle Pierce were crouching down, and my brothers were motioning for me to follow them out of this curving canyon, exiting by following the longer path back to the community. We were not going to attempt to climb up the icy cliffs, and I was very relieved to know that.

I assumed my dad and Uncle Pierce were going to make a run for it, as soon as my brothers and I were some distance ahead of them. I began to walk, being as quiet as I possibly could, aware of every tiny crunching sound my shoes were making. I was about halfway between the guards who were sleeping near the fire and the guards who were over near the path when someone started yelling.

"Hey! You can't just get up and go like that! You have to stay here! Come back here!"

Instinctively, I started running after my brothers, hoping we would be able to get by the other two guards before they were fully awake. Aches and pains all over my body were threatening to slow me down, but the adrenaline of fear kept me going. I could feel someone's breath on the back of my neck, and that helped me to go even faster. As I approached the two guards, coming up behind David and Daniel, those guards stepped back to let us pass.

"You kids can go, we don't care, if you want to be out here in the dark like this, with all the snakes and vultures," a guard shouted at us.

I began to wonder if this community used the phrase 'snakes and vultures' to keep people under control, but I kept running just the same, until we were safely out of this circular canyon. To my surprise, my brothers circled around me and ran back to where the guards were now going after my dad and Uncle Pierce. I turned to watch what was happening back there while continuing to walk backwards, to increase my distance from the guards. I realized my brothers and my dad had planned how to manage this escape.

"You leave my dad alone!" my brother shouted at the guards. "You are going to be in big trouble if you don't let him go!"

"This is not the prince we have here," a guard said. "These two men are troublemakers, and we were instructed to keep them here. If they decide to comply with all the rules, they will be able to return to the community in three days."

"No, that is my dad, and you have to let him go!"

"I am not going to disobey my orders, like some people around here do," the guard said accusingly.

"I know who you are, and I am going to tell on you, and you are going to be called a troublemaker, and you are going to be sent out here if you don't let my dad go!" my brother threatened.

While the guards were arguing with my brothers, my

dad and Uncle Pierce slipped by them in the darkness, unseen.

"You are not about to get me in trouble, you little manipulating monster!"

"I am going to tell the Queen what you called me!"

The guards were getting in a scuffle with my brothers as my dad and Uncle Pierce caught up with me.

"Keep running," my dad said, and we took off at top speed along the well-traveled path. By now, the moon had come up, conveniently lighting our way.

"What about David and Daniel?" I asked, worried about my brothers.

"You don't need to worry about them," my dad said.

"They can certainly take care of themselves," Uncle Pierce added.

We turned a corner so we were out of view of the fire and the guards, but my dad would not let us slow down.

"Keep running," my dad urged.

"My legs… (puff-puff) are… (puff-puff) so… (puff-puff) tired," I said.

"We have to keep running," my dad said.

"You and Uncle Pierce… go on ahead of me…" I said. I really needed to change my stride to a walk. "You run as fast as you can… to get away… because… it doesn't matter… if they catch me. They… don't… want… me."

"We can't leave you alone out here," Uncle Pierce said. He wasn't even breathing hard.

"I will keep following you," I said, slowing my pace, "and Daniel and David will probably catch up with me soon."

We were out in the desert, the bare desert, well-lit by the moon, without even a cactus or bit of sagebrush to hide us, and a long, uphill path ahead of us. Even from here, I could see that it was a much longer path than the one my brothers and I had taken earlier this evening.

"We have to keep running, Layla," my dad said, putting his hand at the small of my back to give me a little push.

"Just think about your mom, waiting for us," Uncle Pierce suggested.

That thought gave me a boost for about thirty seconds, although I was sure he was anticipating Aunt Moon at the end of our marathon.

My dad began to sing a song I had not thought about since I was a little girl, a song about the goodness of God:

With God I can go higher,
With God I can go far,
With God I can move mountains,
Because He keeps me in His care.
In His care, in His care,
Because He keeps me in His care,
I will never need to worry,
Because He keeps me in His care.

The tune and the words stirred something within me, and I felt myself being transported back to the time when I knew and believed the lines of this song. When Dad got to the third line, 'With God I can move mountains,' I joined in, singing with him. We kept running while we were singing, running and singing, and, without knowing how we got there, we were at the top of the hill and back to the point where the path had branched into two. We stopped running and I marveled at how we had gone from all the way down there to this place up here, without my sore muscles bothering me, not even one time, and how the distance seemed to shrink while we were singing about God's power to help us.

I looked down the path behind us, and although the moon was just about down to the horizon, I could see that nobody was following us up here.

"I wonder, which way do we go from here?" Uncle Pierce asked, as he looked down the paths at our two choices.

"We go this way," I said, pointing to the way my brothers and I had come.

"Are you sure?" Uncle Pierce said.

"How do you know?" my dad asked, as we were catching our breath.

"This is the way David brought Daniel and me, and we went up that way to get to the cliffs above where you were," I explained.

"At least we will be going slightly downhill," my dad said, as we began to walk down the path that would eventually lead to the secret entrance to the palace.

"I wonder where David and Daniel are now?" I asked, as soon as my heartbeat had returned to its normal rate.

"They will probably get back there before we do," my dad said. "They know their way around here, and how to get wherever they need to go."

"David does, but I don't think Daniel knows his way around out here," I said.

Just then, we were startled just about out of our skin.

"Boo! Hahahahaha!"

My brothers appeared out of nowhere! I did not see them coming, but they were right there, in front of us.

"We took a short cut," David said casually. Even in this short time, I was already able to tell the difference in my brothers' voices. Daniel's voice had an uptight edge to it, while David's voice was more confident and indifferent.

"Yeah, we had to climb a mountain," Daniel complained.

"It was just a little hill," David said, getting in the lead and turning around to walk backwards so he could face us.

"You made me climb a mountain! It was huge!" Daniel whined.

"It was nothing. We made it, didn't we? Don't be such a baby."

"I am not a baby! I am two minutes older than you are!"

"Yeah, and you will never let me forget it."

"What happened to those guards?" I asked.

"Guards? What guards are you talking about?" David asked.

"The guards, back there, the men who were guarding Dad and Uncle Pierce."

"Oh, those guys. They will be fine," David said. "They won't be bothering us anymore. At least not for a few days."

"Why, what did you do to them?" I asked, a bit worried.

"We just reminded them of some things they needed to remember," he said with a laugh.

"Yes, some things they needed to remember!" Daniel said.

"How much farther do we have to go?" my dad asked.

"We should be there in about a half an hour," David said, "if we keep walking this slow."

"The sun will be coming up soon," my dad said, picking up the pace a bit. "We need to have a plan. How are we going to get into the palace?"

"Oh, that won't be a problem," David said. "What might be a problem is if Mom is still in the isolation chamber."

"Isolation chamber?" my dad asked, with a note of panic in his voice. "Why would your mother be put in an isolation chamber?"

"It is not really an isolation chamber," Daniel said. "That's just what Davy calls it when the princes take our mom and her sister into their chambers, because we can't go in there. Everyone is locked out of there, and they are locked inside, until the princes want to come out. We never know how long they will want to stay in there."

"We have to get them out as soon as possible," I reasoned, "because they have to know their wedding was no good."

"That is an excellent way of putting it," my dad said. "That wedding was not a real wedding!"

"With all the beautiful ladies in this community, why did the princes choose to marry Mom and Aunt

Moon?" I asked, sure that my dad and Uncle Pierce were wondering the same thing.

"Because of us," David said.

"You are so arrogant!" Daniel said.

"You don't even know what 'arrogant' means!" David snapped. "You just said that because you heard someone else say it!"

"What do you mean, David?" I asked. "Because of you?"

"Because the princes want heirs," David said. "We are the only kids, so they want to be able to pass their royalty down to us."

"I heard Mom say that it is really sad that our community is dying out," Daniel said. "No babies have been born here, but lots of people have died."

"Weren't you born here?" Uncle Pierce asked.

"No, we were born somewhere else, but Mom doesn't ever talk about it," Daniel said.

"Some people from here were out scouting and they found us, Mom and her sister and Jasper and us, in the place where we were living, and they brought us here when we were little," David explained. "Then, just awhile ago, everyone decided to have a Queen and so her two sons became the princes, and the princes needed wives and heirs, and since no one here can have children, the princes had to marry our moms."

"How do you know all that?" Daniel asked.

"I told you, I listen to everyone, not just the old people they have who tell you stuff," David said.

"So the Prince does not love our mom?" I asked, stuck on the idea that people who got married should be in love.

"I don't know," David admitted. "Mom loves us, and that's all I care about. She told us that no matter what happens, she will always love us."

"Everyone loves the princes," Daniel added. "Everyone wanted to marry them, all the girls, I mean."

"Yeah, everyone except Mom and Aunt Moon," David said.

"Well, the wedding was meaningless, because both brides are both already married," Uncle Pierce said. I thought I heard a tone of relief in his voice, the same relief I felt when I heard David admit that Mom did not love the Prince she was forced to marry.

"The wedding was meaningless because it was not even a wedding," my dad added. "It was just a form of celebration. God was not in it."

"Dad, how did you know that bride was Mom?" I asked. "Her whole head was covered and you couldn't even see her face."

"A man doesn't have to see his wife's face to know his own wife," my dad said. "I could tell by the way she was standing, and the way she was moving, her mannerisms."

"She wasn't even moving!" I said, trying to understand.

"You couldn't see it, but I could," my dad said. "A husband knows his own wife."

"Uncle Pierce, did you know it was Aunt Moon?" I asked. "Before Dad said anything, I mean?"

"I had been searching through the crowd for her," he said, "and we had a good view of everyone from where we were standing. I knew she was there, somewhere, but I didn't see her in the crowd. I began to notice something familiar about one of the brides, and I was pretty sure she was Moon. When your dad shouted, then I was positive that was my wife standing up there."

We were approaching the secret entrance to the palace as the landscape was coming into view with the rising of the sun.

"Everyone in the palace is still asleep," David said. "We can get in there with no problem. No one will see us."

"Where are we going to go?" my dad asked.

"We can go in my room," David said. "No one ever comes in there. You can sleep on my couches, if you want, and I will go and find out if Mom is still locked up, or if we can see her."

I felt a huge leap of my heart with those words, 'we can see her.'

"We can go to MY room," Daniel said. "It is not as messy as David's room is. He never cleans it."

"I can't waste my time," David said. "How do you think I know things? Not by staying in my room and cleaning it up, I can tell you that!"

We followed him as he climbed down the stone steps and around the huge rock. Ahead of us was the enormous door, the secret entryway into the palace. He pulled the door handle to open the door. We followed him into the dark hallway, around a corner and down several flights of stairs. He opened a door and motioned for us to follow him. This hallway was well lit. We silently padded behind him until he stopped in front of a door.

"This is my room," he whispered, so quietly that I could barely hear him. He pushed the door open and stepped inside his room.

I was right behind him, with my dad and Uncle Pierce behind me and Daniel bringing up the rear. His room was huge, enormous, with high ceilings and couches and chairs here and there, not in any order or formation. I was expecting to see clothing strewn all over the place, but the room was surprisingly neat. It was also very bright inside, with the sun reflecting off the golden rim across the canyon and shining in the room.

David was looking around the room with a strange look on his face, a look of being unsettled.

"What's the matter?" I whispered.

"Something is not right," he said quietly, as he touched one of the couches.

"You are right about that, young man!" a stern voice from another room shouted.

CHAPTER 18

"Mom!" David shouted, with a note of alarm in his voice. "What are you doing here?"

"Where have you been all night?" my mom demanded.

I stood there, dumbfounded, as my mom and my Aunt Moon entered the room, followed by the two princes and Jasper.

We all stood there for about four years, it seemed, looking at each other in disbelief, before anyone spoke.

"We shall have you removed for making trouble," Prince Arumbo said, looking at my dad and Uncle Pierce.

"Didn't we already do that?" Prince Botolo asked. "I know who you are! You two are the troublemakers from the wedding. You will not get away with this." He made a move to leave the room, supposedly to fetch a guard or something.

"No, wait!" my mom said. She moved slowly, so slowly, in a dreamlike manner toward my dad who was standing there, frozen. "Obiad?"

"Pierce?" Aunt Moon said, from across the room. "Now I know I am still dreaming." She fell onto one of the couches and Uncle Pierce rushed to her side.

"And who is this little man?" he said, as Jasper joined them on the couch. Uncle Pierce wrapped his arms around both of them and hugged them tightly.

Aunt Moon was crying. "This is our son, Jasper. Jasper, this is your father, your real father."

"No!" Prince Botolo shouted. "I am now his father!

We had the wedding, and Jasper is my son now!"

"You can say what you like, but he will always be my son," Uncle Pierce said, as he held his family protectively.

"Obiad," my mom said again, stepping over near my dad. "I thought I was imagining your voice today. When I heard your voice, I thought God was speaking to me from heaven, telling me not to go through with the wedding. Then I blacked out."

My dad reached out to hug her, but Prince Arumbo grabbed her away from him.

"This is MY wife, and these are MY sons, and you can't do anything about it!" Prince Arumbo shouted, sounding like a spoiled child. "And, Sun, for your information, the wedding was yesterday, so we have been married ever since then."

"The wedding was a farce!" my dad said. "Sun is already married to me! We have been married for nearly twenty years!"

A group of men came running into the room.

"Take away these two troublemakers!" Prince Arumbo shouted, pointing to my dad and Uncle Pierce. "And this time, take them farther! This is their second offense! We do not tolerate second offenses!"

"Wait!" I shouted. Up to this time, I had been standing in the room unnoticed. I still had a scarf wrapped around my head, covering my crazy golden hairstyle. "Don't take my dad away!"

All eyes were upon me. Nobody moved. I looked directly at my mom as the recognition dawned on her face. Now she began to cry.

"Who are you?" Prince Arumbo asked. "I have never seen you before, and I know every female in this community!"

That statement kind of creeped me out, but I held my head high. "I am Layla. This is my dad, these are my twin brothers, and this is my mom."

After an instant of silence, my mom broke loose from Prince Arumbo's hold and leaped over to hug me.

"Layla? Layla!" She pulled the scarf from my head. "What happened to your hair?"

"Hahahaha! It's all smashed now!" David said.

"Some artistic stylist got a hold of it," I said.

"You!" Prince Botolo said. "You were the one who cause the panic at the celebration!" he said accusingly. "I was looking right at you and your hair was lighting up beautifully."

I shook my head. "No, I was about to tell my mom who I was and right then all the trumpets or whatever began to sound, and everyone started going crazy," I said.

"This was all your fault!" Prince Arumbo said, stepping over close to us.

"I did it!" Daniel shouted. "I pushed the panic button!"

Everyone looked at Daniel. "You are always the good boy, Daniel! You never do anything wrong!" my mom said.

"This was not wrong," Daniel said.

"We did the right thing, for our family," David added.

"You certainly did," my dad said. He opened his arms and my brothers, my mother and I went into them for one long-overdue family hug.

a novel by Dana Pride

A global disaster, known as The Great Devastation, drastically changed life on earth. Layla, a Kidgen, or Kid-Genius, is living and working at the Complex, where the Insiders have everything they need provided for them: jobs, food, clothing, entertainment. Layla is aware of the Outsiders, (the Ordinaries, the Crims, the Chairs and the Runners) who are just scraping by without the use of technology, but she doesn't have any reason to think much about them - until Kenrick, one of her friends who is also a Kidgen and a Comgen (Computer-Genius), secretly arranges for four friends to travel.

Suddenly Layla becomes curious. What is life Outside really like? Where will they go? What will they eat? Will they be able to get back safely and unpunished? Kenrick has a few surprises in store for them, especially for Layla, whose life will never be the same after they make their journey Outside the Complex.

Also available from Everlasting Publishing:
the second book of The Great Devastation trilogy:

Layla's journey with her father continues...

a novel by Dana Pride

Now that Layla has found her father, she attempts to settle into his primitive lifestyle and the culture that has adopted him. As soon as she meets new friends, she tries to help them, inadvertently causing the entire group to begin another adventure. While they are forced to move quickly from one place to another, they learn about the existence of others who have survived The Great Devastation; as Layla and her father are drawn toward a great discovery – and eventually, the truth.

Books available from Everlasting Publishing